The Elle Project

Printed in the United States of America

First Printing, 2021
ISBN: 9798485622466

Editing by Jenn Lockwood
Cover design by Summer Dowell

To my six children,
who taught me anything can be done in the
midst of chaos with enough determination and
peanut M&Ms.

Table of Contents

Chapter 1 - Elle

"Chestnuts roasting on an open..."

I jam my finger against the radio dial.

Nat King Cole can take his roasting chestnuts and shove them down his own throat this frigid morning. Clearly, he's never had to scrape ice off his windshield with a credit card or drive a car so old its heater only works at about fifty-percent capacity.

On the bright side, if an apocalypse ever comes, my body knows how to survive glacial weather. I practice every day during my work commute.

As I pull up to a red light, my phone vibrates in its dashboard clip. One day, I'll own a car new enough to have Bluetooth technology. That day has not come yet.

My mom's name flashes across the screen, and even though I'm not in the mood for family gossip, I know if I don't answer, she'll call me every fifteen minutes until I finally do. Sighing, I tap the speaker button.

"Hey, Mom." The muscles in my jaw have been frozen shut, and I hope she appreciates the effort I'm making to get them moving. "How's your day going?"

"Elle, you have no idea the turmoil going through our house this morning!" my mom exclaims, ignoring my greeting. "Your dad forgot to set his alarm clock and was an absolute grouch until I got him out the door. And then, in the middle of a load, my washing machine stopped working. Just poof! I'll tell you if I..."

I slowly zone out. My mom—bless her heart in that ironic way southerners say it—can make an avalanche out of a snowflake.

The light turns green, and I hit the gas. Although, considering there's a layer of ice on the road that's just waiting to give someone an insurance claim, what that really means is I speed up from zero to fifteen mph. Watch out, Daytona 500.

I slide one hand under my thigh, hoping my body heat can stave off the frostbite.

"...and since Oliver's going to stay in town, I told Dad that we could—"

Her words are like a jolt of electricity. "What?"

She pauses for breath—something that hasn't happened for five minutes—then says, "The sprinkler problem? I think the leak started in the flower beds."

"No, Mom, not the sprinkler. What did you just say about "—I swallow like it's not a struggle to get the name out—"Oliver?"

"*Oliver*? Did I mention Oliver?" Her voice turns shrill. "I'm pretty sure what I said was, um, *olives or* cheese. You know I'm still trying to come up with a charcuterie board for Christmas dinner. How do you feel about Gruyere? Auntie Sharon keeps telling me it's a great table cheese."

"Mom." My mother may have missed her calling as a professional filibusterer, but there's no way her mindless chatter is going to work on me.

She's quiet for a moment, and I can almost hear her wheels turning. "Now that I think about it, I might have mentioned Oliver's name. He's such a darling boy, you know."

"Mom, he's a twenty-nine-year-old man."

"Ah, time does seem to fly these days. Anyway, back to Christmas, when will we be seeing you?"

I hold in a groan. Getting a straight answer out of this woman is like finding where they keep toothpicks in a grocery store. Impossible. "Is Oliver Moore going to be home this Christmas?"

"I mean, I don't know his schedule verbatim."

If my mom doesn't know the exact hour he'll arrive, I'll eat my hat—if I had a hat.

"However, his mother *may* have mentioned something about him being in town for the holidays."

I don't even try to hide my groan this time. "Ugh, no. Mom! You guys set this up, didn't you? You and Lauren?" Oliver's mom, Lauren, and mine have been next-door neighbors and best friends since I was in diapers. I have no doubt as to the level their scheming could go this Christmas break. I glare at the festively decorated shops I'm driving past. Holidays. They ruin everything.

"I don't know what you're talking about. If it just so happens that Lauren decided to request her son stay home this Christmas, what does it matter to you or me?"

"Because you know as well as I do that Oliver *always* spends Christmas with his dad—ever since we were in high school." I grip the steering wheel like I'm trying to wring its neck. "And doesn't it seem ironic that this is one of the first Christmases in the last five years *I've* been able to come home as well?"

"Elle, who am I to complain when fate deals us a blessed hand? Now, since we're speaking of Oliver, can we discuss your vacation wardrobe? Please pack something suitable. Something besides those baggy sweatpants or—"

"I'm hanging up. I will call you back when I've given time for my anger to simmer down—if it ever does!" I holler into the speakerphone.

"Wonderful, dear. I'm glad we've had this chat. See you next week." My mom's cheery voice would have you thinking we just discussed the weather.

I glare out my foggy window. Not my weather. Hawaii's weather.

Oliver Moore is going to be home this Christmas. Of all the holiday tragedies that could happen, it had to be this.

Leaning forward, I jab the button to turn off my phone with all the frustration in my body. What I don't realize is that my coat sleeve has caught on the edge of the steering wheel cover. As I bring my arm back to my lap, my trapped sleeve turns the wheel with it, jerking the car toward a cement divider to my right.

Screeching, I overcorrect and yank my arm to the left, which means I'm now drifting toward a giant truck that is probably some guy's midlife-crisis purchase—the kind where the hubcaps are level with my passenger window.

I'm going to die.

Using the adrenaline rush to my advantage, I wrench the sleeve of my coat with a strength my personal trainer would be proud of. And when I say personal trainer, I mean the steroid junkie that helped me during the free fitness session that came with my gym membership. It sounds better when I don't explain it.

Snap!

The noise, along with the fact that I now have my hands at their proper ten o'clock and two o'clock positions, confirms that my sleeve has escaped its trap. My heart is racing like an ultramarathoner, and that is actual sweat trickling down my back despite the cold.

It takes about five more seconds of deep breathing before all my other senses start functioning again. That's when I hear it.

Beep! Beep! Beep!

Is somebody honking at me? I look around the winter wonderland that is my life, ready to glare at whatever jerk is trying to add to my problems. All I see are curious eyes staring back at me.

My gaze drops to my steering wheel, and there's a flat piece of plastic with a few frayed wires where my horn button is supposed to be.

Oh my gosh. That's me. That's my car honking.

The light in front of me turns red, giving me a second to assess what's going on. My hands scramble over the dilapidated wheel, metal wire tips pulling sharply against my fingers.

Where is the emergency off button? Shouldn't there be a switch somewhere?

The red light turns green, and I have no choice but to start driving again.

And that's where I am, cruising through work traffic at a wicked fifteen mph, honking at the driver in front of me every five seconds.

This is one of the most embarrassing moments of my life.

I completely blame Oliver.

*****

Two hours later, I've thawed out with the help of a subpar cup of hot chocolate and my mini space heater. Sophie, my best friend and cubicle mate, insists the thing makes our office as dry as the Sahara desert, but I appease her with a new hand lotion every few weeks. And by appease, I mean she usually rolls her eyes at my generous three-dollar offering.

At the moment, though, I'd give just about anything to be back at that desk, battling the desert heat, instead of sitting here having a *chat* in my boss's office.

Chats. That's what he likes to call these meetings where he lectures me on my most recent mistake.

The armchair I'm in has far too many brass tacks and far too little cushion, but I hardly notice since I'm perched on the edge. My boss, Thompson—who has a last name for his first name?—sits in front of me, a patronizing smile on his face.

"Elle, you know we pride ourselves on excellence here at Keller Accounting. We are nothing if not top-notch service. So, can you please tell me why your tic marks on the Wells Grocery account are all in blue?"

He flips his laptop around as if I have no idea what the spreadsheets I've been working on for the last week look like.

"As the preparer, you understand your markings are supposed to be in red, correct? How will the reviewer know which ones are his and which are yours?"

I slip one hand under the opposite arm and pinch the soft skin there as a reminder to keep my cool. "I apologize, Thompson. I do know the color system." *Breathe in through the nose, out through the mouth.*

"As you probably remember, this was Darren's project that I took over." Darren, the senior manager who'd given his two weeks' notice then spent his last fourteen days researching condos in Miami instead of finishing his projects. "Since Darren started out using red, I figured it would be more efficient to just continue with his system rather than go back and change all his tics." I am so glad I got a four-year degree so I could sit here and discuss color options with my boss.

His hands come forward, interlacing those chubby fingers on his desk. "Of course, and I can see how someone of your"—he pauses in that way people do when it's completely unnecessary, but they're trying to make you feel inferior—"experience level would think that."

I pinch myself harder. I will not break. I will not.

"But regardless of the circumstances, you do realize I expect you to follow protocols, even if it means a little more work?"

I nod. I'll agree to just about anything to get out of here.

"All right, you're free to go, just next time—"

I don't wait to hear his advice for next time. Considering it'll be something along the lines of choosing royal blue instead of sky blue, it probably doesn't matter.

Sophie's eyes shoot to me as I slump into my desk chair, pity written across her face.

"That bad, huh?"

"Be careful what colors you use on your spreadsheets," I say, opening my laptop. "Thompson is channeling his inner interior-design skills this week. I recommend sticking to a nice crimson or rust for your edits."

A grin is already sneaking across Sophie's face. "I heard Tammy got in trouble last week for using the wrong date formatting. Two-digit years instead of four."

I shake my head, my irritation still too fresh to laugh. I try to click open my emails, but the mouse has frozen on my screen. With an annoyed huff, I slam it onto the laminate desk, hoping I can shock it back into usefulness.

Sophie eyes me over her monitor. "You doing okay? You've been a little on edge all morning."

I smack my mouse once more, but my defibrillator attempts aren't bringing the thing back to life. "I haven't had the best day," I say, leaning back in my chair.

Sophie mimics my position. "Tell me everything. I've been listening to this meditation app every night the last two weeks, so I'm basically a certified therapist at this point."

I snort and bring my feet up to rest on the seat in my chair. Sure, I'm wearing a skirt, and anyone who comes around the corner might get flashed, but I don't even care at the moment. "You know about my horn debacle."

"Hmm, yes. That was rather unfortunate, but Dave was able to turn it off for you, right?"

Dave, a well-known car junkie who works in sales, did some magical voodoo on my horn and got it to stop beeping. Now let's just hope I never have to use the thing, because I have no idea how to turn it back on. "Yes, but that's not all. Do you remember the neighbor friend I grew up with? Oliver?"

Her eyes narrow like she's trying to place him.

"You know, my next-door neighbor. The one my family has been attempting to set me up with since we hit puberty? The one my mom insists I'd make beautiful babies with?"

"Oh, *that* Oliver! What's wrong?" She wiggles her eyebrows. "Is somebody else having his baby?"

I roll my eyes. "Get your mind out of the gutter."

"Hey, you brought it up."

"My mom informed me this morning that Oliver is going to be home for Christmas."

"Which is bad because...?"

"Which is bad because Oliver *never* spends Christmas at home. He always celebrates it with his dad in Washington."

She gives me a blank look.

Seriously, has this girl never read an Agatha Christie book? Where are her deduction skills? "Coincidentally, this is the first Christmas *I'll* be home in almost five years. Don't you think it's a little suspicious?" I wave my hands in the air. "Some underhanded activity is going on by our mothers."

Her scrunched face relaxes. "Ah, I see. So, you think this is some sort of romantic setup. A forced-proximity scheme."

I forgot that Sophie is a huge Hallmark fan. "Yeah, something along those lines but less serendipity and more scheming aunties. Anyway, I don't know if I'm mentally ready for the onslaught of matchmaking efforts that are going to happen this week. Maybe I should just pretend to be sick and say I can't make it."

"Oh no, this is the first Christmas in almost five years you haven't been doing an end-of-the-year inventory count. You have to take it. Do it for those of us who are going to be holed up in some warehouse, counting handbags for Macy's or something."

I laugh. It's true. I love my job as an auditor, but there are some downsides, like the mandatory, year-end job of proving inventory for our bigger companies. I've finally reached a senior enough position that I can pass that off to others.

"What's the guy's name again? Oliver?"

Sophie's hands are on her keyboard.

"Oliver Moore." She's looking him up on social media. I wait for it.

There's some more typing and then, "Elle! What the—" She's found him.

"This? *This* is the guy you're avoiding? This is the charity project your family is cruelly trying to set you up with?"

Her eyes are as wide as those cinnamon rolls from the bakery next to my apartment—the one I visit way too religiously. What can I say? I support small businesses. And sugar.

"What the heck, Elle? If you don't want him, I'll take him. He's a total babe!" Her nose is inches from the screen like it will help her get a better view of his pixelated face.

I blow out a breath of air. "Yeah, well, I never said he was ugly. Just that I didn't want to marry the guy."

"Call me shallow, but usually those things go hand in hand." Her eyes finally leave the monitor. "I don't care what his hang-ups are. My posterity would benefit from having that jawline in their gene pool."

I drop my feet, and despite the fact that I have every hair on his head memorized, I can't help leaning forward to glance at her computer. Yep, he hasn't changed his picture. It's still one of him standing on a giant, manly looking excavator machine—the kind his landscaping company uses.

My eyes dance over his features. He really is the epitome of handsome with that naturally bronze skin that no tanning lotion has ever been able to achieve for me. His broad shoulders and contrasting trim waist make you wonder if he has to get all his shirts tailored to fit so well. He has dark hair that's always a tad long, like he's due for a haircut but hasn't quite gotten around to it, and there's one wavy piece that always falls in his eyes—

Geez. Pull it together, Elle. I lean back and look away. "See, this is why I didn't want to show you his picture. I knew you would be taken in by his good looks." *Ah, hypocrisy is a funny thing, isn't it?*

"Excuse me for having a thing for a perfectly dimpled smile and eyes the color of chocolate. Call me crazy, but—"

"Can we get back to me? You can have your fantasies about Oliver on your own time." I straighten my shoulders and force all my own fantasies out with a mental riot shield.

Sophie turns her chair to face me with dramatics that should be in Hollywood. "Fine. I'm ready." One hand reaches out to turn off her screen. "Hit me with all the reasons why Christmas with your Greek-god neighbor is going to be so terrible."

"It's going to be terrible because I'm going to be surrounded by my family." My mind goes to the chaotic group of people waiting for me on Bluffdale Lane. If it was just my parents and siblings, I could probably hack it. My mom is a little over the top, but my dad stays out of the drama. Sure, my three brothers get a little annoying, but I can deal with a few snide remarks and nudges here and there. The problem is, it's not just them.

Two doors down is my Auntie Sharon—a woman whose gossiping capabilities make my own mom look like a saint. Auntie Sharon was married to my dad's brother who died ten years ago due to heart complications. She still has two children, though. A daughter named Jenny, who's been running an orphanage in Africa for the last three years and is engaged to a doctor. (It is wonderful to be compared to unremarkable achievements like that.) And a son named Logan, who is luckily as average as me in both his love life and career.

If Auntie Sharon isn't enough, next door to her is my Auntie Lisa, who's married to my dad's second brother, Uncle Marlo. Uncle Marlo, like my dad, is one of the few relatives who prefers to stay out of everyone else's business. On the flip side, his wife does not share his preferences. It really is amazing that my dad and his brothers—overall quiet and reserved men—managed to marry such extroverted women. My only saving grace is that Auntie Lisa has two sons in high school keeping her busy, so my love life is relatively low on her list of to-dos.

"Ah, come on." Sophie kicks her heels up on her desk. She's wearing slacks today, so there's no worry about flashing the world. Lucky girl. "What's the worst that could happen?"

"Please, don't jinx me with a question like that," I say and drop my head into my hands. "It's not so much what they might do—although that's definitely a boundless list. It's just the fact that they all think I'm their little project. In their heads, Oliver and I are perfect for each other. We're a match made in heaven. And I hate that. I hate that they're all just sitting around with their bowls of popcorn, waiting for us to put on a show for them. I just want them to mind their own business and leave me to mine."

Sophie chews one fingernail, her eyes studying me.

"All right, out with it. What are you thinking?"

Her eyebrows lift. "What makes you think I'm thinking anything?"

"You're biting your nails, and you're looking at me, but your mind is a million miles away. You're clearly thinking of something."

"All right, James Bond, now that I know I'm being watched by a spy." She drops her hand and focuses on me. "I'm just wondering if maybe you have it wrong. Maybe your family's ultimate goal isn't to prove that they know you better than you know yourself." She shrugs her shoulders. "Maybe they just have your best interest in mind. What if Oliver really is the perfect match for you?"

My mouth drops. "You too, Brutus? You haven't even met him, and you're already on their side?"

She throws her hands up, the motion rolling her chair back a foot. "Look, I'm on no one's side. And by the way, it's *et tu brute*—c'mon, haven't you ever watched *Aladdin*? I just know that if my family tried to set me up with a man worthy of becoming my screensaver, I wouldn't be putting up this big of a fight."

With a final snort, I turn my chair back toward my computer. "Trust me, my family has no idea what's best for me."

Chapter 2 - Oliver

I'm singing along to "Frosty the Snowman" as I pull into my mom's neighborhood. Well, at least I sing along to the first three words of the song, which happen to be the only words I'm sure anyone knows.

Regardless, the music combined with the blowup Santas and reindeer littering most of the snow-covered lawns is giving me the jolt of Christmas spirit I need.

I was initially hesitant when my mom requested I stay home for Christmas instead of heading out to my dad's. Although, *requested* is rather misleading—more like *commanded*. She threw in the fact that I'd missed Thanksgiving this year, which was no fault of my own since she was the one that booked a trip to Hawaii over the holiday, but it's amazing how much guilt a mom can still draw out of you even after thirty years of life.

Regardless, here I am, pulling up to the curb of my childhood home, feeling a moment of nostalgic bliss come over me. This was a good decision, a little change up to my normal routine is just what I need.

And then I see my mom.

She's standing on the sidewalk, one hand on her hip, the other flailing about wildly. Next to her is Tammy, her neighbor and best friend for the last thirty years. Tammy's hands are clenched under her chin, her eyes riveted on my mom. Ten bucks says they're thirty minutes into a good gossip session.

I consider pulling away, maybe circling the neighborhood for another half hour until they're done, but they've spotted me, and all hope is lost.

"Oliver!" my mom squeals like I've come back from the dead. Like I don't live less than twenty minutes away, and we didn't just talk on the phone the night before. And when I say *we* talked, what I mean is, my mom talked, and I listened while watching highlights on ESPN. The blessings and curses of being an only child.

I step out and wrap my arms around the petite bundle of maternal energy. "Hi, Mom. Good to see you."

A second later, another set of arms comes at me from the side, and I recognize the bracelet-lined wrists as Tammy's.

"So good to see you, Oliver. It's been forever."

Again, the exaggerations are a little much considering my landscaping business just revamped Tammy's house two months earlier. Meaning, I spent weeks literally in her backyard every day.

I get one arm around her and give her a tight squeeze as well. "Hi, Tammy, it's good to see you too."

And I mean it. Growing up, Tammy was like a second mom. She went to as many of my sporting events as my own mom did, always had a listening ear, and fed me better than she did any of her actual children.

"This is perfect timing," Mom says, giving me a mischievous smile. "I was just thinking about taking Buzz out for a walk, but now you can do it for me."

Buzz is my mom's golden retriever—the one I strongly voted against her buying a year ago as a puppy. I suggested she get something easy, like a hamster or, better yet, a goldfish. But my mom had gotten it in her head that she needed a companion, and apparently, nothing but a seventy-five-pound shedding machine would do.

"Great," I say, knowing there's no way out of it.

"Aren't you looking dapper these days, Oliver," Tammy cuts in, her narrowed eyes sizing me up. "I don't suppose there's any special girl in your life, is there?"

My mom elbows her friend, her eyes widening. I can almost see the silent communication. It's like their own language of eyebrow raises.

"Of course there's not, Tammy," Mom says. She turns a suspiciously bright smile on me. "But speaking of successful, attractive young women..."

Were we speaking of that?

"...Tammy was just telling me that Elle is going to be in town for Christmas this year. Isn't that a pleasant surprise?"

And that's when the pieces fall into place. It's like finally hitting that ketchup bottle in the right spot, and all the sauce drops onto your plate in one breathtaking glop. Elle. That's the reason Mom insisted I stay in town this Christmas. That's why she called to confirm I was still coming not once, not even twice, but three times this last week. As if I had hoards of other Christmas invites I was considering.

I try not to groan out loud. "Elle's going to be in town?"

This might seem a little dramatic. Who wouldn't be excited to see one of their childhood friends? Especially someone who was like a sister. But that's the point. Elle isn't my sister. The gorgeous, vivacious woman is not in any way or shape related to me. And that's the trouble.

When we were little, there weren't any problems between us. Her older brother, Noah, was one of my best friends, and Elle loved to tag along with us wherever we went. It didn't take long before the Carter family felt like my own. And when I say the Carter family, I mean *all* the Carters. I mean Auntie Sharon who lives on the other side of my mom's house with her two kids. I mean Auntie Lisa and Uncle Marlo and their crew two doors down. I mean every birthday celebration, Fourth of July BBQ, graduation celebration—you name it—my mom and I were there, part of the gang.

I think they initially felt sorry for us. There I was, an only kid with divorced parents and my mom trying to raise me on her own. I'm sure our family situation looked pretty sparse compared to their rambunctious lot. They were more than happy to be my quasi siblings and cousins.

And then I hit puberty.

It was around my fourteenth birthday that I distinctly recall looking around and noticing Elle was a girl. An attractive girl.

I still remember studying her across the table as everybody sang me an off-tune version of "Happy Birthday." She was wearing a faded pair of overalls and had a giant red-and-pink scrunchie holding back her long hair.

She was the most beautiful thing my fresh fourteen-year-old eyes had ever seen.

After that, things got weird between us. It was like one day we were friends, kicking the soccer ball around at the park, and the next day, Elle would no longer talk to me.

I'd come by the house to watch a game with her dad and brothers, and she'd immediately go upstairs to her room. Her mom would invite us over for Sunday dinner, and she'd be the first to leave the table and offer to wash the dishes. Heck, we even had a biology class together my senior year where she purposely sat across the classroom, refusing to even make eye contact the entire semester.

It was too bad my teenage hormones refused to accept her blatant rejection. Elle was on my mind constantly, even though I did my best to pretend I didn't notice her. I was a living, breathing male after all, and Elle was one of those girls that hit puberty early. Let's just say I wasn't the only guy sending her covert stares in between classes.

It didn't help that there'd been an obvious push from both our families to get us together. When we were little, it was funny when our moms would say things like, '*Elle and Oliver are going to get married, and we'll be grandmas together!*' At the time, we made the appropriate disgusted faces, gagging at the very idea of marriage. The teasing became a lot less funny when we realized exactly what making them grandmas entailed.

As her siblings and cousins got older, they joined in the subliminal—and some not-so-subliminal—teasing about getting the two of us together. I laughed and tried to put on a smile most of the time, but Elle never dealt with it well. It usually ended with her stomping off to her room, red-faced and vowing to give everybody the silent treatment.

When the day came that I flew the coop for college, I'm pretty sure we both gave a sigh of relief. Since then, we've only seen each other sporadically when our trips home line up—something I'm confident Elle purposely avoids.

The last time I laid eyes on her was at her brother's wedding, four years ago. And no, I definitely don't still have the image of her that night (dressed in a low-cut black dress that disrupted my sleep for at least a week afterward) and the preppy loser (I mean, the gentleman wearing a too-tight suit and a pink dress shirt) she brought imprinted on my mind. I just happened to really like the cake they were serving that night, and I associate her with that memory.

"Oliver?"

I snap out of my dream-induced state to see my mom and Tammy staring at me with curious looks. "Huh? Oh, yeah, Elle's coming home. I'm so...excited." Excited to get the cold shoulder from her along with the never-ending winks and nudges from family for the next week.

With a sigh, I head toward my mom's front door. "I'm gonna take Buzz for his walk." At the last second, I turn back to Tammy. "When is Elle supposed to get here?"

She gives me a smile that has way too many expectations in it. "In the morning."

Great, so I have twelve more hours to set up my internal anti-Elle attraction barriers.

Chapter 3 - Elle

I fold up a dark pair of jeans, ignoring the memory of my mom telling me to bring something appealing. I'm not packing these jeans for Oliver. And I'm definitely not packing that fitted V-neck or my favorite slinky green dress for him either. I just want to be prepared for any event.

I eye the heaping stack of leggings and oversized sweatshirts. I'm packing those for him.

The alarm on my phone goes off, my reminder that I need to get out the door in the next ten minutes to make it to the airport on time. I shove the remaining clothes into my suitcase and can only zip the thing up once I sit on top and use my body weight to compress everything.

It's only as I'm pulling on my shoes that I realize I forgot to pack underwear. Groaning, I eye the already overstuffed bag. Maybe I can just shove some into the outside pockets?

As I roll the cotton fabric into tiny cylinders that will hopefully fit, my mind wanders to the week ahead of me.

All previous plans of spending time with my family, binge-watching Hallmark movies, and eating my weight in sugar cookies have been overshadowed by the fear of what they have cooked up for Oliver and me. What sort of matchmaking schemes will they resort to?

For not the first time, I wish Oliver's and my relationship was different. I wish those awkward high school years—the ones where I could barely even look at him without a blush exploding across my face—had never happened.

Although, to my defense, my family sure hadn't made it any easier. It was around my fifteenth birthday that everyone decided it was time to lay down plans for Oliver's and my future matrimony. I couldn't go anywhere without someone making an embarrassing comment or trying to push us together. It got so bad that during my junior year I started dating Miles Grover, a senior who wore way too much cologne and had an obvious love affair with his biceps. It was a sacrifice I was willing to make, though, just to get people off my back.

I still remember the haunting way Oliver looked at me the one time I brought Miles home for a family party. It was the first and last time I ever did it. And since everyone spent the entire evening interrogating Miles about his life goals and future plans, it was no surprise when he broke up with me a week later.

My family can be a little intense.

No, things between Oliver and me have always been weird. And despite what my family thinks, there never was and never will be anything romantic between the two of us. And they only have themselves to blame.

My snoozed alarm goes off again, and the first miracle of Christmas happens when I am able to zip the outside pocket of panties closed.

Two minutes later, I'm out the door, more resolved than ever to put Oliver behind me.

*****

"Don't worry, I got it," I say to my Uber driver who looks like he's not a day over fourteen.

He watches as I heave my massive suitcase out of the trunk, and I think he's more concerned about his paint job than me pulling a muscle.

I'm questioning how this bag passed the airport's weight limit when it finally drops to the street with a thud. I force myself to stop panting and give him a smile. "All good. Thanks again."

He stares once more at his bumper then shrugs and heads back to the driver's seat.

Well, at least there's one person this Christmas vacation who didn't pester me with questions. As a matter of fact, I don't think we said more than two words to each other the whole drive. Maybe I should stay with him for the next few days.

My eyes flicker up to my house then over to Oliver's. Is he here yet? I should've asked my mom exactly how long he'd be in residence on Bluffdale Lane.

I wonder if he's changed at all. Looks-wise, I know he's as attractive as ever—thank you, social media—but is he the same Oliver? Does he have the same easy-going personality he's always had? Oliver was the kind of guy who had a smile for everyone and could make any situation seem funny. I wonder if life has jaded him in the last few years.

I like to think that I've changed, matured over the years, but a small part of me hopes Oliver hasn't.

As I'm in the middle of these deep, introspective thoughts, I hear a shuffling noise from behind me. Spinning, (literally—there's some slick ice on this road) I come face to face with the man himself crossing the street.

Holy cow. He's ten times better in person than on the screen. I drink him in like a glass of mulled apple cider. The kind where you know someone was a little heavy-handed with the cloves, because it gives you a heady kick right after it warms you to your toes.

He's dressed in loose jogger pants and a fitted T-shirt that seems to be a passive-aggressive protest to the knee-high banks of snow around us this morning. My eyes spend an embarrassing amount of time studying the abs and chest that are somewhat visible despite his shirt before moving up to his face. Brown eyes that are so dark they're almost black are watching me under heavy brows, the silent stare making me catch my breath.

Then, he smiles.

Familiar, deep laugh lines that he had even as a kid spread across his face. Dimples you want to reach up and slide your thumb across to see if they're real appear, and I momentarily cannot recall why I ever moved away from this gorgeous man.

"Hey, Elle—"

Before he can finish whatever articulate greeting he's about to give, a mound of golden fluff comes leaping at me.

"Buzz!"

Despite Oliver's yell, the fluff continues to bound forward, its mouth wide open.

Assuming these are my last moments, I cower with my arms braced in front of my head. If I'm going to die, at least I'm going to be buried with my face fully intact.

Regrets flood my mind. I should've told my mom I loved her more. I should've thanked Sophie for always being a good friend. I should've told Oliver—

Riiiiip!

I peek between my fingers, wondering if I've been bitten and the pain just hasn't registered yet, when I see a flurry of pastel fabric flying through the air.

I spread my fingers wider.

Wait. That's not fabric. That's an entire week's worth of underwear scattering across the driveway.

My underwear.

Maybe death wouldn't be so bad after all.

"Buzz!"

I hear Oliver's voice again and realize he is yanking the suitcase-attacking furball away from me by its collar.

In a flash, my senses come back, and I spring into motion. I'm dashing around like a madwoman, grabbing panties out of the air and off the ice-crusted ground. I'm Doctor Octopus—nothing can escape my whirling arms.

As I'm diving for a final, particularly embarrassing red pair with pink hearts all over it, my fingers collide with Oliver's massive hand.

I look up to see he's holding a sunshine-yellow pair and a lacy black one as well. Apparently, my Doc Oct impersonation isn't as good as I thought.

"Um, I think these are yours," he says, offering the traitorous panties to me.

I snatch them out of his hand, only slightly mollified to see that his own face is at least half as red as I'm sure mine is. His other hand is holding the mischievous animal back, although I can see the dog is straining at the edge of his leash, still going after my bag.

"Buzz, stop, you moron!" Oliver drops his gaze back to the animal, and I take a moment to admire the way the muscles in his forearms are trying to get the excited golden retriever under control. A vein pulses in one of them, and I'm fascinated by it. What body-fat percentage does someone have to have to get pulsing veins in their forearms?

"What's going on here? Buzz, come here, boy." Lauren, Oliver's mom, steps out of my house with my own mother in tow.

Really? Really, Universe? Why don't you just drop an anvil on my head while you're at it?

"Elle, you're here! And Oliver, you're helping with her luggage? What a gentl..." My mom's words trail off as she gets close.

I know what this looks like. Actually, I have no idea what this looks like. It's not every day I scatter my unmentionables across my parents' driveway. But I assume it looks questionable.

"Elle just arrived, but Buzz decided to attack her luggage, and things got a little...uh...messy." The blush on Oliver's face deepens to a dark crimson.

I didn't realize speaking about a woman's underwear would embarrass him so. I would've tucked that information away for future use if I wasn't planning on spending as little time as possible with him on this trip.

"What? Buzz, you naughty little doggy," Lauren says in a voice you'd think would be reserved for cute babies, not pantie-attacking monsters.

I jam the traitorous underwear back into any available nook and cranny in my luggage. I don't care where it goes at this point; I just want it out of sight.

"I'll take Buzz up," Oliver says, tightening his hold on the dog's leash. He turns back to me. "Sorry again about this, Elle. I hope he didn't ruin anything."

I give him a tense smile that's mostly for my mom, who is staring at me expectantly. "No worries, everything is good."

He nods and jogs up to his mom's front door.

And then it's just me and the matchmakers.

"Goodness, Elle, that tactic did seem a little forward, but I admire your boldness." My mom widens her eyes at me.

A giggle escapes Lauren. "Back in my day, only a certain type of woman threw her panties at a man."

The two of them burst into laughter, and I know my smile has turned into a grimace. Despite my expression, my mom reaches forward and pulls me in for a hug. "I'm just glad you're finally opening up to him," she says, giving my arms an extra squeeze as she steps back.

"Mom, I did not throw my panties at him. The dog ripped open my suitcase, and Oliver was just helping me pick up my...items." I pop up the handle of my bag, determined to go inside and lock myself in my room for at least the next twenty-four hours. "And I don't know what you mean by 'opening up to him.' Oliver and I are the same as always. Cordial neighbors."

Mom does this eye roll combined with an eyelash flutter only she has mastered. "Please, I've been waiting for you to set your cap at that boy for years. Don't tell me I have to wait longer."

I place my fists on my hips, determined to end this once and for all. "Mom, I am in no way, no how setting my cap at Oliver. Both because I have no interest in him"—words that have no business in my mouth rush out—"and because I am happily involved with another man." Wait. I'm what?

Silence. Blank looks and silence.

"Y-you're involved with someone? As in, you're dating someone?"

I don't know why an announcement like that should produce so much shock from the both of them.

I straighten my shoulders, grabbing the suitcase handle with stiff fingers. "Yes, Mom. I have a boyfriend. Which is one of the many reasons why there will be no romantic connection between me and Oliver." Not having the energy to continue discussing this fib I concocted thirty seconds ago, I head up the driveway. "I'm going to go unpack."

I can't help wondering if this will be the most genius lie of my life or the most troublemaking.

*****

"I need your help. I just told my whole family I'm dating someone."

"But you're not dating anyone."

Sophie's voice comes in loud over the phone, and I immediately shut the speakerphone off. You never know where listening ears might be in this house. "I know," I say, whispering now. "That's the point. I lied, and now I need you to help me cover my lie."

"Why are we whispering?"

I roll my eyes and flop onto the floral comforter that now covers my childhood bed. My mom wasted no time transforming my room into her formal guest room. The only hint left of me are my bins of knick-knacks she's stored away in the closet. "Because your voice is loud enough for everyone in my neighborhood to hear, and I'm trying to discuss a secret operation with you."

"Like 007 style?"

Yeah, if you take out the expensive gadgets, swanky clothes, and the ability to have a perfect comeback in every scenario. "Basically." I roll onto my side, eyeing the suitcase I still have to unpack. "While it may be a lie, it's really the simplest way to get everyone off my back this week. I can't believe I didn't think of it earlier. I can't date Oliver if I'm dating someone else."

"Do you have someone lined up to play this fake boyfriend?"

I chew my bottom lip. "You."

There's silence for a second before she responds. "While I am flattered, Elle, I think we both know that I am not interested in you in that way. It's nothing personal—"

"Stop being a dork, Sophie. I don't mean for real. I mean you're going to help me fake like I have a boyfriend." My mind quizzes with options. "It's not like I actually need a guy. I'll say he went home to his family for the holiday or something. I might just need some proof that he's real. You know, like maybe I'll call you on the phone, and you can pretend to be him. Something like that."

"I don't know. This sounds like one of those cliché romantic comedies. The ones where someone pretends to be in a relationship, and everything ends in a metaphorical train wreck."

"What are you talking about? Romantic comedies always end with a happily ever after. This plan is foolproof!" I'm waving my arms now, and I've dropped all pretenses of whispering.

"And what exactly is the plan? You saying sweet nothings to your boyfriend that doesn't exist? Will you call him—me—in the middle of Christmas morning as proof to everyone?"

She's really killing the vibe of this thing. "I don't know! It's a work in progress. I just need to know you're on board in an emergency." I'm back to my whisper tone. James Bond would be so proud.

She sighs, and it's one of those long dramatic ones that makes you wonder if there's any air left in her body. "Fine. I'll help. But I still don't think this is a good idea. You know what *is* a good idea is getting together with that gorgeous childhood friend of yours."

"That's why I am the idea generator and you're the facilitator in this operation." I slide off my bed, landing in a heap next to my suitcase. Might as well tackle this thing while I'm talking.

"Fine, fine, call me whenever you need some pillow talk."

"Ew. I will call you if I need to have a normal conversation with my imaginary boyfriend."

"Roger that. Alpha is out."

"We're not part of the military, Sophie."

"Tango Bravo."

I roll my eyes. "Goodbye."

"Terminating."

I click the disconnect button before she can shower me with any more of her terrible spy terms. As my fingers grab the outer zipper of my suitcase, I realize Lauren's dog bent it. Good thing I never liked this bag.

I make quick work of dumping out my stuff, instinctively organizing my clothes into cute outfits and ugly loungewear.

I can guarantee my mom and Tammy have spread the word that I'm dating someone. Those two have gossip radars that move at the speed of light. The key now will be to play it off as well as possible, which makes me a little nervous considering I was one of the few kids in seventh-grade drama that got hand-picked to be part of the stage crew—and it definitely wasn't because of my technical abilities.

I flip my suitcase over to make sure I got everything out when a wrapper drops from the outer pocket. I reach down and pick up an empty package of beef jerky.

Of course. No wonder that furball was attacking my suitcase like a maniac. This must've been left in my bag from my last trip.

Feeling a little less vengeful at the animal, I finish organizing my clothes at a snail's speed. Anything to put off facing the music downstairs.

It's only when I've folded my socks and underwear into the most perfect crisp lines that I accept it's time to move on.

Taking a deep breath, I open my door and head downstairs.

Chapter 4 - Oliver

I've decided the key to this vacation will be to spend as little time as possible at Elle's house, which is a pretty unfeasible task since she's only been home for forty-five minutes, and I've already been texted twice by her brothers to come over and watch the game.

I can only use the excuse that I'm taking a shower so many times before people get suspicious.

Drying off from my shower—might as well take one after all—I stare at my open suitcase, wondering which T-shirt I should wear. It's a stupid question. They're all the same, just in different colors. But for some reason, the decision seems important. Elle is over there.

Sighing, I grab the navy-blue one on top and shove it over my head. Technically, I didn't need to pack for this week since I only live about twenty minutes away, but I figured it'd be easier having everything here so I didn't need to keep driving back and forth from my place to Mom's.

Now I wish I had a reason to make that twenty-minute drive, if only to buy myself more time. I throw on a pair of jeans and finger-comb my hair into something I hope looks presentable. For a split-second, the idea of wearing cologne runs through my head, but then I think of Elle's brothers and realize that's just asking for some ribbing.

Heading out the door, I sprint the fourteen steps over to their patio. Sure, I could've put on a coat, but then I'd just take it right off again, so the effort seems pointless. I give my cursory warning knock, which I realize two steps in was wasted, given the volume levels in here.

A smile creeps across my face. I've missed this. I've missed the Carters' crazy, in-your-face family dynamics.

Out of habit, I slip off my shoes and shove them under the entryway bench that's already housing a hoard of sneakers, slippers, and snow boots. After passing through the photo-lined hallway, I reach the back where the noise increases tenfold.

I take in the wide-open space that serves as the Carters' main gathering place.

Across the room, Elle's twin brothers and at least two cousins are lounging in every possible way across the massive sectional couch, watching a game. Their dad, Drew, is seated on a La-Z-Boy with one eye on the screen and one eye on the book in his lap. Elle's Auntie Sharon is at the breakfast nook, her phone pressed to her ear, her mouth and free hand moving nonstop.

Then, my eyes drift to the area I'm purposely avoiding: the kitchen. The spot where Elle and her mom are working side by side on some kind of cookie bonanza.

Elle's back is to me. She's wearing some fitted black leggings that I'm sure are innocent and casual to her, but the way they hug those curvy legs is casually bringing my heart rate up. And now I'm suddenly curious about which underwear she has on. I wonder if it's that black, lacy pair.

I swallow and make a silent commitment to keep my eyes shoulder-level and above.

She turns, and her profile is now in view. Thick lashes are aimed down at the counter where her hands are working. I don't even need to see them to remember those green eyes. They're the kind that you don't really notice until she wears green, and then they pop out so much you wonder if she's part leprechaun or something.

Her hair, a brown that's light enough you know she was blonde as a kid, is thrown up with some velvet-looking scrunchie in what I'm pretty sure girls call a messy bun. The way it bares her long neck makes me think I should have a few more messy things in my life.

"Oliver, honey, come in!"

While I've been busy ogling her daughter, Elle's mom has spotted me hovering in the doorway.

I force my mouth into a smile and lean against the doorframe. Like, look at me, so calm and nonchalantly pretending my pulse is beating a standard sixty beats per minute.

"Hi, Tammy." I nod toward the TV across the room. "Just checking the score to see if I want to watch this game." *Yeah, sure, buddy.*

She seems to buy my lame excuse and waves her hand at the screen. "Football, schmutball. Come have a cookie; you're too skinny. I just cleaned up lunch if you want a sandwich."

I'd feel flattered, but Tammy tells everybody they're too skinny. It's her indirect way of forcing people to eat the food she's made. I walk to the kitchen, but only because of the rows of cookies laid out, not because it puts me one step closer to Elle. "No, I already ate. But wow, are you guys feeding the whole neighborhood cookies?"

Tammy sends me a wink, but Elle just continues piping green frosting onto a Christmas tree. Her mom gives Elle a not-so-subtle nudge with her hip.

Apparently, I'm not the only one who noticed Elle's lackluster response.

Okay, fine. There was no response whatsoever.

"It's so wonderful you stayed home for Christmas," Tammy says. "We were thrilled to hear the news, weren't we, Elle?"

Elle finally looks up. "Thrilled," she deadpans.

Tammy doesn't seem to notice as she throws one hand up with a dramatic flair. "Oh, no. I forgot to switch the laundry over to the dryer!" She backs up, her eyes ping-ponging between Elle and me. "I'm just going to go do that for a few minutes. Elle, you finish these cookies and catch up with Oliver. Ask him about work. Or how his fantasy teams are doing. Maybe what movies he's watched lately? His mom mentioned he'd just seen—"

"Mom!"

With an extra pep in her step, Tammy whips out of the kitchen, no doubt to return from her fake task and spy on us in about thirty seconds.

I pluck a snowman-shaped cookie off the counter just to give myself something to do. "Is everything okay with your suitcase?" I ask because we all know there's no way Elle's going to ask me what new movies I've seen. "I'm sorry again about Buzz. I don't know what got into him."

Instead of looking mad, she gives a halfhearted shrug. "Yeah, it was my own fault. There was an empty bag of beef jerky in the pocket. I'm sure that's what he was going for."

I nod and break off Frosty's hat. "That makes sense. I have a hard time passing up beef jerky too."

She sends me a smile so brief I'm not even sure if it happened, then she goes back to her cookies.

This is going well. "So, how's work?"

"Still plugging away."

"You always did love numbers."

She nods. "Still do."

"How's Denver?"

"It's good."

"That's nice." Painful. That's how I would describe this conversation. I pop the hat into my mouth, trying to come up with my next approach. "So, do you—"

"Oliver! Get away from those womenfolk, and come watch the game!"

I'm not sure which twin is responsible for the ridiculous comment—I think it's Brett—but both of their faces are staring at me from the other side of the couch.

"Bring us some cookies while you're at it!"

That was definitely Rhett.

"If you want any of these cookies, you can walk your butts over here and get them yourselves," Elle hollers back, not even sparing her brothers a glance.

I'm already on Elle's bad side with the whole underwear incident, so I head to the couch sans cookies.

"Chicken," Rhett mutters as I drop down next to him.

He's the only one gracious enough to move his legs so I can have a seat, so I spare him a cutting retort. "What did I miss?" I ask. They spend the next ten minutes giving me conflicting summaries about the first two quarters.

Drew finally cuts in to his sons' argument about which side the refs are favoring. "How's work going, Oliver?"

"Yeah, I've been meaning to ask you about my petunias. They've seemed a little dry this week." Brett snickers and fist bumps Rhett right before I give him a dead arm.

He moans and grips his shoulder like a baby while his brother and cousins laugh hysterically.

Elle's little brothers' favorite pastime is giving me grief about my landscaping business. According to them, I spend my days singing to sunflowers and watering daisies.

"Work is good," I say, addressing Drew. "Things are always a little slow in the winter, but I've got a bunch of designs we're working on for spring."

We chat for a few more minutes about his own redesigned yard, discussing the putting green Tammy never approved of and therefore never made it into the plans.

"So, Oliver, did you hear about Elle?" Rhett asks.

I sit back and throw my hands behind my head, keeping my eyes on the screen to make sure he knows I am not interested in whatever he wants to tell me (which is a lie—I'm 100% interested in anything that has to do with his sister). "Hear what?"

Now the rest of the guys are leaning in, which makes me leery. I get the feeling this is information they're not supposed to share.

"Oh, it's nothing too interesting." Brett stretches out, his feet landing on the well-worn coffee table in front of us.

"I mean, it's not like anybody in this family really cares about her relationship status or anything."

Before I can stop them, my hands drop, ruining the nonchalant vibe I'm going for.

Rhett and Brett both give me this maniacal twin grin, and for the thousandth time, I wonder why their parents gave them such ridiculously similar names. They know they've got me with their stupid bait-and-switch comments.

"If you don't want to tell me, I don't care," I say, my mind going through every relationship status that could be possible. She could be dating someone? Maybe she broke up with someone? Maybe someone broke up with her? Maybe I need to go break a few bones of whatever punk broke up with her?

Before I can start looking up revenge tactics, Rhett breaks in. "It seems like our sister is—"

"Oliver, where did you go?"

Tammy has made her way back into the kitchen and must have realized her daughter and I are not in the process of confessing our true love as she had planned.

I lift my head over the couch and give her a wave. "Hey, Tammy, just watching the game."

She gives me a flick of her spatula, a silent command that I am not man enough to ignore.

I leave the safety of the overstuffed sofa with a back slap from Brett and an apologetic look from Drew. We all know none of them would ignore a command from Tammy either.

Elle is purposefully ignoring my gaze again as I walk up to the counter. I notice she's moved on from Christmas trees to icing gingerbread men.

"Oliver," Tammy says as she begins drying dishes. "I want to know how your business is going. You know Drew and I are so pleased with how our yard turned out." She sends a not-so-sly glance toward her daughter, as if to double-check she's listening. "Have you heard how well

Oliver's company is doing, Elle? I'm so impressed with what he's accomplished on his own."

"You're very nice, Tammy." I go to lean on the counter but realize every inch is covered with cookies. "Things are going good, overall. Winter can be a little slow, but it should pick up again in the spring."

"Don't be modest." She turns back to Elle. "Did you know Oliver's company won the award as the Best Business in Sandpoint this last year?"

I feel my face heat up. "It was actually just Entrepreneur of—"

"Can you believe it? You know, he built this thing from the ground up." She gives me a broad smile. "Such dedication and hard work can only be admired."

Don't think I don't see what this is. I feel like I'm twelve years old again, interviewing at my first job with my mom hovering over my shoulder, attempting to convince the manager I'm trustworthy enough to hand out newspapers.

Elle finally looks up, and I see it—the crack in the facade she's trying so hard to keep in place. The outside corners of her eyes are squinting slightly, and she's biting on the inside of her cheek to keep that smile down.

It's not much, but it's enough to make me relax a little.

"Yes, Mom. Oliver has always been very successful at whatever he puts his mind to." Her words are for her mom, but her eyes hold mine. "I'm sure he will live a very long and prosperous life if he keeps this up."

I'm not as strong as her. A laugh begins to escape me, and I grab a plain, star-shaped cookie and shove it in my mouth.

She cocks one eyebrow. "I haven't iced that one yet."

"I'm starting a new diet," I say, my words muffled around the buttery concoction. "It's a no-frosting diet."

Her lips part, and I see a hint of perfectly straight teeth that I happen to know took four years of braces. "Wow, I admire your commitment. A weaker man would've stopped at just no sprinkles, but you took it all the way to frosting."

"Sacrifices must be made sometimes."

And I've done it. Her mouth breaks open in a wide smile, and an unmistakable snort leaves her.

I've almost forgotten her mom is standing three feet away, watching. "You two always did get along so well," she says, her eyes questionably shiny. "Elle, did you know that Oliver still comes over and mows his mom's lawn every week? You know, it's not every day you find a man with dedication like—"

"Are these cookies done yet?"

I rarely appreciate an interruption from one of the twins, but in this case, it's welcomed. Rhett reaches past me and grabs two snowmen, somehow managing to devour one in two bites.

"Did you even taste that?" Elle asks, going back to her frosting.

"Of course. But just to make sure, I grabbed another one." Rhett shoves the second cookie in his mouth, and it meets its demise as quickly as the first.

"He's a growing boy, Elle," Tammy cuts in, giving Rhett a motherly smile. "Here, honey, take a few more."

"Mom, he's almost twenty-five years old. If he's still growing, then we've got bigger problems on our hands."

Rhett rewards Elle by chewing big messy bites with his mouth wide open.

"Ew, I can't work with that in my vision," she says, shoving him back.

Her brother laughs and turns to me, slapping one arm on my shoulder. "I was just telling Oliver the good news when you called him over." He tilts his head toward me, but his eyes stay locked on Elle. "Elle here has got herself a boyfriend back in Denver."

I know this is done mostly to get a reaction out of Elle, but my whole body freezes up when I hear those words. I think I'm trying to smile, but I'm like Dorothy's Tin Man who needs a serious shot of oil to get his joints moving again.

Elle has a boyfriend? I know it's ridiculous to hope she'd remain romantically unattached the rest of her life, but the thought of her with another man makes me sick enough to regret every cookie I've eaten.

"You never mentioned why your boyfriend didn't come home with you for Christmas." Rhett's having the time of his life. "You aren't ashamed of us, are you?"

I finally get the nerve to see how Elle's reacting. She looks calm. If it weren't for the fact that she's squirting frosting on the counter instead of the cookie in front of her, I'd say she's completely unaffected.

"He couldn't come," she says, her jaw stiff like she needs a shot of oil too. "His work is super busy right now, and he couldn't get away."

Rhett nods and keeps mowing through the line of sugary snowmen. "Really? What does he do? It must be something important to not be able to take time off for Christmas—especially for his girlfriend."

Half of me wants to cover my ears and pretend this conversation isn't happening, and the other half is hanging on every word. Yeah, who is this guy? Who's the man Elle's deemed worthy enough to claim a place in her life? For as long as I've known her, which is basically forever, she's always shied away from serious relationships.

Not that I've been keeping tabs on her. I simply happen to hear things through the grapevine, is all. And the grapevine has informed me the only real boyfriend she's had was back in her senior year of college. And even that wasn't serious, at least according to Tammy—I mean, the grapevine.

"He does have a very important job. Not that it should matter to you." Elle has noticed her frosting mishap and is trying to scoop up the mess with a paper towel. "But if you have to know, he works in management. For a managing company. He's very busy...managing things."

"I'm getting the feeling you don't know what your boyfriend does."

I'm glad Rhett said it, because there was no way I was going to.

"I do, too, know what he does." Elle drops her paper towel mess in the trash then sets her hands on those hips that are ever-so-nicely defined by those black leggings.

Eyes up, Oliver.

"He's a project manager for an events management company. They manage lots of...events for companies. Which is why he's not here. He's managing corporate Christmas parties right now."

I'm still about fifty percent sure she's lying, given that she's said *manage* at least ten times in the last minute, but I can't figure out what she's lying about. Why would she lie about her boyfriend's job? Maybe he doesn't have a job?

Rhett is not having this. "What, like he's a party planner?"

"Okay, leave your sister alone." Tammy comes around the bar and grabs her son by the arm. "Why are you trying to ruin everything?" she asks in a whisper that is definitely not a whisper. "Elle and Oliver are finally catching up, and you come and—"

"So work is good?" Elle asks, her loud question obviously an attempt to drown out her mom's voice.

I nod, still thinking about this boyfriend of hers. "Yeah, everything's going good."

"Oh, my heavens, customer service these days is ridiculous!" Elle's aunt slams down her phone on the dining room table before making her way toward us.

I'd almost forgotten she was in the room.

"What's the matter, Auntie Sharon?" Elle grabs her frosting and goes back to decorating.

"You know those couches I ordered last month? Come to find out..."

And that's when I slink my way back to the couch, my head filled with more questions than I want to count.

Chapter 5 - Elle

I should've never come home. The second I found out Oliver would be here, I should've made up an excuse. I got mono. I drowned in a hot tub. Anything.

He's been at my parents' house for four hours, and it's been a cruel mix of heaven and torture. Although, to be fair, most of the torture is being inflicted by my brothers and mom. Oliver can take full credit for the very sparse heaven moments.

I look toward the table where he's been talking with my Auntie Sharon about her flower beds for almost twenty minutes. A lesser man would've broken by now, but not Oliver. He's still smiling and sweetly answering every question she has about the soil's pH level and whether singing to her flowers really does help them.

He nods at her last comment, lifting one hand to rub what is probably two days' worth of scruff lining his jaw. On anyone else, I'd guess it'd been at least a week since they shaved, but Oliver has always had superhuman hair-growing abilities. Even as a teenager, he could've had a full beard if he'd wanted to.

What most people don't know is that if you catch him right after he shaves, when there's nothing but smooth skin on his jaw, you realize he has a total baby face.

Not that I'd know or anything.

I shift on the couch and try to focus on the TV. Although, considering this has to be at least the third football game today, it's a struggle to stay interested. I have no idea how I'm going to last three more days in such close proximity with this man. Surprisingly, I survived eighteen years of living next door to him without caving to my feelings, so you'd think a few days would be nothing.

He throws his head back and laughs, and suddenly, I find myself counting how many times those dimples appear. One. Two. Three.

That whole *'absence makes the heart grow fonder'* saying might have some merit.

I shift again, propping a pillow up on the right side of my head—for comfort...and maybe because it blocks the very cliché tall, dark, and handsome man from my view.

Actually, the real thing that's bothering me is the fact that no one in my family believes I have a boyfriend.

When I first came downstairs, I was met with a room of expectant faces, everyone wanting to know the details about this mysterious guy I hadn't yet mentioned. I'd been able to deflect most of the questions and suspicious looks, but then Rhett had to go and make everything worse by cross-examining me in front of Oliver.

Not that Oliver could care less if I have a boyfriend. He's probably grateful that I got everyone off our backs. I just wish I'd come up with a more solidified version of who my fake beau is before Rhett's inquisition—as in, where he works and what his name is.

I need reinforcements. I pull out my phone, hiding it between my legs.

Elle: I need help!

Sophie: Are you getting mugged? Why are you texting me?! Call 911!

Elle: No, not like that. Geez, why would I text you if I was getting mugged? I mean boy drama.
Elle: No one believes my fake boyfriend is real.

Sophie: Sorry, I've been watching crime documentaries lately and am in the middle of

researching how many deadbolts you can install on a front door.

Sophie: Also, your fake boyfriend isn't real, so they're right.

Elle: Whose side are you on?

Sophie: I'm sorry your family thinks your pretend boyfriend is just pretend. How can I make this better?

I can hear the sarcasm through her words. Luckily, it's not enough to stop me.

Elle: Can you call, pretending to be my boyfriend?

Sophie: Really? Are we going there? I thought you were kidding when you said that.
Sophie: Also, how's McDreamy? Can you take a picture of him and send it to me?

Elle: Do you know how stalkerish that sounded? No. I'm not taking a picture of him to send to you.

Sophie: A true friend would.

Elle: A true friend would help me out. Call me in two minutes, pretending to be my boyfriend.

Sophie: Speaking of stalkerish...

I set my phone aside, my palms already sweating as I eye my surroundings. This really is the perfect setting if I'm going to stage a fake call. Everyone of importance is in the room. And by importance, I mean everybody who won't stop pestering me about Oliver.

My twin brothers are on the far side of the couch, taking turns yelling at the TV. My cousin Logan, the same age as the twins and almost equal to their annoyingness, is sprawled out next to me.

My mom has joined Auntie Sharon, and now they're in a deep discussion about my cousin Jenny and approximately how long it'll be before she and her fiancé start producing grandbabies.

And then there's Oliver. He's still at the table with my mom and auntie, looking perfectly at ease, as if he's simply lounging in his own living room with his own family. Which, to be fair, is how we've always treated him. Another reason why he and I will never be compatible. You can't get romantically involved with someone you've grown up thinking of as a brother.

A very hot and charismatic brother with whom you happen to have no actual blood connections.

The vibrations of my phone make me jump almost a foot in the air.

Logan looks over at me with raised eyebrows. "You okay?"

I ignore his question and lift my phone up. "Look, it's"—*crap, what was the fake name I'd decided on?*—"Danny!" Great. All I have to do is call myself Sandy, and we could do a reenactment of *Grease.*

I don't know if it's my words or the volume of my voice projecting across the room, but all eyes zip to me.

I wave my cell in the air like a trophy. "It's my boyfriend, Danny." Giving my brothers an especially simpering smile, I bring the phone to my ear.

"Hey...baby," I say into the cell, only slightly tripping over the cringe-worthy endearment.

"Oh my gosh. Don't call him baby. Nobody's going to believe this is real if you try to pull off a pet name like that."

Sophie's voice rings in my ear, and I thank the heavens she has the sense to whisper. As much as I want to argue that I'm totally the type of person to use a pet name for her boyfriend, I smile and say, "Aww, I miss you too! What are you up to?"

"Well, I was just about to leave this prison we call work for lunch. Going to treat my overworked brain to a greasy fast-food burger and milkshake." I can hear shuffling noises on Sophie's end.

"Work's busy? You think you'll be there all night again? I'm so sorry. I wish they didn't need you so much." I look around at my rapt audience as I say this, my eyes wide as if to say, *See? My boyfriend is super busy managing all sorts of things in his management position.*

My brothers and cousin are giving me narrowed looks, and I don't know if I'm strong enough to check out my mom's and Oliver's reactions.

"What can I say, not everyone has inventory-counting abilities like me. Some people stopped going to school after third grade." Sophie's monotone really isn't helping me create the lovey-dovey mood I'm going for.

"What am I doing?" I lean back into the cushions, reaching up to play with my hair as if I'm so carefree and happy to be talking to my significant other. "Oh, just hanging out with the fam. Wish you were here."

"I wish I were there, too, so I could be sitting across from that foxy neighbor boy—"

Sophie's reply is cut off by Logan leaning in close. "Are you even talking to anyone?"

I scowl and mouth the words *be quiet* to him. Now Brett is leaning in, and they've both burst any hint of the personal-space bubble I am trying to maintain.

"Yeah, she's talking to someone," he says in a voice loud enough that it would've embarrassed me had I actually been speaking to my boyfriend. "The phone's lit up still."

I jab my finger in his stomach in a very loving way, and he jumps back.

"You should have him video chat so we can all see him," Auntie Sharon says from the table.

"What a great idea!" my mom cries next to her, clapping her hands excitedly. "I want to see Danny."

For the billionth time in my life, I wonder why I have such an overbearing extended family. Panic sets in, and my fingers dig into my cell.

"What? They want me to video chat with them? I don't think my acting skills can stretch that far, Elle," Sophie says, no longer whispering.

I shake my head at my mom and aunt, but now the whole family has clung on to the idea. "Yeah, we want to see this man who has swept you off your feet, sis." Rhett has a teasing glint in his eyes.

My gaze finds Oliver, probably the only sane person in this room. He's watching me with pity in his eyes, a look that says he wants to help but has no idea how to.

For a moment, my heart clutches, and I wonder why the heck I'm doing all this. Why am I working so hard to resist any appearance that I might be interested in this man?

I hear the front door slam, and a second later, my Auntie Lisa walks in.

"What's going on?" she asks the room that is riveted on me.

"Elle is going to video chat her boyfriend so we can all see him," my mom says, still staring at me with expectant eyes.

"I didn't even realize she was dating someone." Auntie Lisa immediately settles in at the table, her eyes bouncing back and forth between Oliver and me.

And then I'm brought back to reality. This is why. This is why I will never pursue anything with Oliver. There are ten sets of eyes staring, waiting for me to ask my co-worker

Sophie, playing the part of my fake boyfriend Danny, to video chat with them.

"What's that?" I say into the phone, digging deep for my best acting skills. "You just hopped out of the shower? Ah, darn it. Okay, I'll tell them." I cover the phone with one hand as if protecting my boyfriend's delicate ears. "Sorry, guys, he just got out of the shower, so he can't video chat right now." I force as much regret in my tone as possible.

"Wait a second, you just said he was at work," Rhett says, walking back into the room with a family-size bag of chips.

Crap. "His work is one of those all-inclusive places," I say, having no idea what I'm talking about. "They have a gym and shower on site." I stick my nose in the air, trying to act offended at his very legitimate question.

"Well, I definitely don't want to see another dude in a towel, so we'll have to video chat later."

I don't think I've ever been more grateful for Oliver's strong baritone in my life. He's sending me a smile from across the room, but I can tell there's confusion in his eyes. Like he knows he's saving my back, but he's not sure why.

Regardless, I am not missing this opening to escape. "You know, I'm going to finish this conversation in my room where there are less distractions," I tell my very captivated audience. "Hang on a second, baby," I say into the phone, once again struggling over that last word. "I'm going to change rooms real quick." I stand as I speak, stepping over all the legs resting on the coffee table that none of the males in my family have the manners to move.

The last thing I hear as I escape up the stairs is my brother's parting shot of, "Give Danny our love!"

*****

I'm still storming about the whole situation twenty minutes later in my room.

"I just know I'm going to think of the perfect comeback I should've said to my brothers two weeks from now." I'm standing in my bathroom, studying my face up close in the mirror because whenever I get agitated, my favorite thing to do is to look for a pimple to pop.

"Yeah, the whole video chat was a curveball we didn't plan for," Sophie agrees, still sympathizing with me out of the goodness of her heart. "Although, I thought you recovered nicely. I'm sure there are lots of companies that have in-house gyms and showers."

"You didn't see their faces. I don't even think my dad believed me, and he's a glass-half-full kind of guy."

"Well, worst-case scenario is having to tell your family you just made it up so they'd get off your back about Oliver. I'm sure they'd all feel so guilty that they'd leave you—"

"Are you kidding?" I give up on finding a good zit and dig through my makeup bag for tweezers. Plucking my eyebrows is my next favorite thing. "Do you realize the ammo I would be handing my brothers if I admitted to something like that? No, I am not giving up now. We just have to be more strategic from here on out. Take an offensive approach instead of a defensive one. Proactive instead of reactive."

"I feel like I'm back on my high school soccer team. Thanks for the pep talk, Coach."

"I'm serious, Sophie. What can I do to add evidence of this boyfriend? What do boyfriends normally do?"

"Exist?"

I ignore her and focus on the baby hairs lining the outside of my brows. "Gifts. A boyfriend would send his girlfriend a gift if they were apart. Flowers?"

"You want me to order you a bouquet of red roses? Do you want the deluxe-teddy-bear-and-chocolates version or just the standard?"

"Obviously, the deluxe, but don't worry about it. I'll just send them to myself. This is good, what else?"

Sophie sighs, and I can tell she's still not on board. "I don't know, maybe you should have a photo of him? Probably one with you in it, otherwise everybody will assume it's a fake."

She's right. I see a big gnarly hair and grab it with my tweezers, pulling hard. "Ow!" Maybe I shouldn't have pulled that one. I rub the tiny gap now visible in my once-perfect arch.

"You're not popping zits, are you? You know that does more damage than good, right?"

"For your information, I am not popping zits," I say, eyeing the sore spot. "I'm plucking my eyebrows."

"Whoa, whoa. Put down the tweezers, and step away from the mirror, Elle. You know the golden rule. Never pluck eyebrows when you're angry. You always overdo it and have to live in regret for the next two months until they grow back."

I love and hate that she knows me so well. "I'm only plucking the strays," I lie, although I do put away the tweezers and return to my bed. "Okay, so a photo. I just need a photo with me and a guy, right?"

"Yeah, a guy your family doesn't know."

Silence fills the space. I know we're both thinking the same thing. I don't have a picture with me and another guy. Why? Because I've spent the last—oh, I don't know—ten years finding fault with every man I have ever gone out with. I have excuses for days.

That guy was too shallow. That one was too quiet. That one was too chatty. Sophie is convinced I have a commitment issue, but I know the truth.

I'm comparing every man to Oliver. Comparing every guy's appearance, personality, and work ethic to the one man I will never allow myself to form an attachment to. The man that I refuse to fall for despite my family's best efforts.

It's easier just to agree with Sophie that I have a commitment issue.

"Didn't I take one of you and my cousin when we went to that concert together?" Sophie's tone is so hopeful it's a little pathetic.

"Maybe." I open my social media app and find Sophie's profile, scrolling down to see her old posts. *Bingo.* "Yes, you're right." I click on the picture to blow it up. "Unfortunately, you're in it too, but at least he's standing next to me." It'll do in a pinch. Not that I had any actual interest in her cousin. His smile was way too wide. Definitely couldn't get in a serious relationship with a defect like that.

"All right, well, as much as I love talking about the finer points of your fake-boyfriend scheme, I need to get back to work sometime today."

I grin. "Thanks, Soph, you're the best. Sorry I'm such a psychotic friend and am pulling you into this mess."

"Any time. And if I ever need to fake a boyfriend in my life, I'll know how to do it after this."

Laughing, I say goodbye.

I spend the next ten minutes researching the closest floral delivery options and trying to decide whether a dozen red roses is too cliché when my brothers burst into my room.

I jump and chuck my phone under my pillow—because that's totally not suspicious. "I appreciate you knocking," I say, my voice only a little shaky. "You two better thank your lucky stars I wasn't standing here naked or something." They both make disgusted faces, Rhett even going so far as to fake gag, which I think is completely unnecessary.

Eventually, they straighten and stand shoulder to shoulder in front of me.

"Dear sister," Rhett says, his voice robotic.

"We came up here to apologize for making you feel uncomfortable while you were sharing terms of endearment with your significant other on the phone." Brett's tone is equally unnatural.

"Yes," Rhett adds. "We hate the thought that we might've embarrassed you in front of your better half."

"Your helpmate."

"Probably your soulmate."

"The future father of your—"

"Staaap," I moan, covering my eyes. I know at some stage my brothers are supposed to grow up and be mature adults, but I'm just wondering if it is going to happen before I die. "Did Mom put you up to this?"

"Yes," they say in unison.

I place one hand over my heart. "No, really, be honest. I hate to think you were concerned about my feelings or anything."

Rhett jumps on my bed, all hints of regret gone as he stretches out. "Nah, you don't have to worry about that. We're also supposed to tell you that Noah and Autumn just got here, and Mom wants you to come down and mingle."

Brett eyes the bed that has been taken over by Rhett and sprawls out on the floor. "To be specific," he says, holding one finger up, "Mom says you are to come down and mingle *after* you put on something a little more attractive." He lifts his head and eyes my leggings and oversized sweater. "Which, I'll have you know, I think you look fine."

Rhett throws a pillow at his twin. "Mom's not concerned about what you think of her." His eyes drift over to me. "However, there is a certain someone downstairs with '*a heart of gold that we can't let escape this family,*'" he finishes in a high-pitched voice that I think is supposed to resemble our mom.

I'm not dumb. I know he's not talking about my brother and sister-in-law that just arrived. He's talking about Oliver. "Out," I say, pointing toward the door.

"Oh, so you're actually changing," Brett says, jumping up. "I assumed you'd ignore that request with all the independent, stubborn vibes you've been putting off lately."

Rhett starts humming Kelly Clarkson's "Miss Independent" song until I shove him off my bed.

"You can tell Mom I'll be downstairs in two minutes, wearing the exact same clothes I have been all afternoon." I brandish a hand through the air to emphasize my comfy outfit. "And Kelly Clarkson was way before your time, so I'm concerned why you know that song."

"I'm a cultured man," Brett says, picking himself up off the floor.

"Out!"

In a perfect unison that only twins and synchronized swimmers seem to be able to achieve, they dash out my door.

I flop back on my bed, my grumpiness from a half hour ago returning. I'll go down there and socialize, but only because I like my sister-in-law, Autumn. It has nothing to do with Oliver or my meddling mother.

Chapter 6 - Oliver

I should've gone home after that phone-call fiasco with Elle's boyfriend, except for the fact that I have zero reasons to go back to my mom's empty home considering she just showed up a few minutes ago. Maybe Buzz needs to go on another walk?

Just as I'm contemplating my escape, a warm little body barrels into me. My arms come around it and lift up the squirming form of one of Noah's sons. "What is this? A little monster for me to eat?" I growl in my best scary-adopted-uncle voice.

"No, no! It's Jack!" The high-pitched squeal of the three-year-old has me grinning. "Don't eat me, Uncle Oliver!"

I tip him over so he's upside down, pretending to drop him before laying him gently on the floor at the last second.

Even though I have zero blood relation to Elle's nephews, they still call me their uncle—a title I don't plan on giving up anytime soon.

"Uncle Brett and Rhett are in the basement with your brother," his dad, Noah, says as he eases next to me on the couch. "Go tackle them." He gives me a spine-cracking back slap as his toddler scampers off. "Hey, Oliver, long time no see. What's new?"

I look over at the man who's been my best friend for the last twenty years. Our friendship has taken more of a backseat ever since he married his wife, four years ago, but considering the whole *'til-death-do-they-part* vows, I'm not too offended.

"You know, just working my way through your mom's cookie platter," I say, nodding toward the half-empty tray that was brought over from the kitchen. I don't want to think about how many I've eaten this afternoon.

We spend the next few minutes catching up on important things like work and why none of our teams are going to make it to the playoffs.

At some point in our conversation, Elle must've slipped back downstairs, because when I look in the kitchen, she and Autumn are leaning on the countertop, laughing. It must be something pretty funny, because that extra laugh line that's on her right cheek only shows up when she's smiling really hard.

Does her boyfriend know that little tidbit about her? I shake my head. He probably knows that plus a lot more.

I must spend too long staring, because Noah asks me, "So, I'm assuming you've heard about Elle's new boyfriend?"

My head snaps back around to the TV. "Oh, yeah, I heard someone mention it." *Yeah, whatever, I might've just casually had a small heart attack when the news was thrown at me, but no big deal.*

Noah leans forward and grabs a cookie. "Rhett and Brett think she's faking it," he says, his voice low.

I choke on the breath of air I'm inhaling. "W-what?" I say, trying to control my wheezy gasps before he gives me another back slap.

One of his eyebrows cocks up. "They think the boyfriend is fake." Now both eyebrows are raised. "That it's a scheme to get the family off her back about a certain someone." He drags out the last words, and I have no doubt he's talking about me.

Sure, we've been teased since before I can remember, but it's not bad enough that she'd make up a pretend boyfriend, is it? As if hearing my thoughts, Elle turns my way, her gaze connecting with mine for a second before flitting away.

"Did you guys know they're lighting up the city hall tree tonight?" Auntie Lisa's voice carries through the space.

"They are?" Elle's eyes light up.

Even across the room, I can see their bright-green color, like fresh-cut grass on a cool morning.

"I haven't seen that in years," she adds.

"But the Potato Bowl is on tonight," Drew says from the La-Z-Boy he hasn't moved from all afternoon.

Noah leans toward his dad. "Did you see the quarterback on—"

"You boys are going to have to get off that couch sometime this week," Tammy says from her perch at the table.

Elle has her hands on her hips. "C'mon, I haven't seen them light up that tree in years. Someone has to come with me."

Tammy straightens so suddenly that I worry she's going to fly out of her chair. Her mouth is pursed, and she's got this calculated look in her eye. "You know, us girls would *love* to come with you, Elle, but we've got that thing going on tonight." She eyes my mom and the two aunties surrounding her. "Right, ladies?" There's a not-so-subtle nod toward my end of the couch, and all four women are now gazing my way.

Auntie Sharon's the first to respond. "You're right," she cries, bringing one hand to her chest. "I forgot all about that."

"Goodness," my mom says, "is that tonight?"

They are dropping like flies.

"I must've forgotten to put it on my calendar," Auntie Lisa finally says, although there's a furrow in her brow like she hasn't quite caught on yet.

Tammy stands, waving her hand at the TV. "That's fine. You boys can watch your game tonight; we'll all be occupied anyway. But who can we send with Elle?" With an arm flare my middle school drama teacher would've killed for, she points at me. "Oliver! *You* can go with Elle! It's been years since you've seen the tree lighting too. You won't mind missing one football game, right?"

I nod, knowing I wouldn't say no if my life depended on it.

Tammy squeals and clasps her hands. "Then it's settled."

Noah leans in next to me and whispers, "Sorry, man. Thanks for taking one for the team."

Little does he know this is not taking one for the team. Spending one-on-one time with Elle feels like Christmas came early this year.

"No." Elle looks like someone just offered her a giant slice of fruitcake. "I mean, that's so kind of Oliver to offer, but"—her arm reaches out, locking onto Autumn's shoulder—"Autumn was just mentioning that she wanted to see the tree lighting tonight."

Tammy's eyebrows raise as she looks at her daughter-in-law. Allegiances are being tested. "But Autumn already agreed to come with us tonight—to our thing."

Autumn gives Elle a weak smile, and we all know she has no choice in this matter. "Uh, yeah. I-I'm sorry, Elle. I've got a...thing."

My mom stands. "Well, if that's the case, Oliver and I better run home and get ready for our outings tonight."

I'm not sure if I'm grateful or annoyed by her intervention. Regardless, I know when to yield and follow her toward the front of the house. As I pass by the kitchen, I look toward Elle and give her a cautious smile. "They light the tree around eight, right?"

She chews her lip but nods.

"How about I come by and pick you up around seven-thirty, then?" I'm not immune to the fact that we have at least eight pairs of eyes watching us, and I feel like I'm asking a girl on a date for the first time.

She visibly swallows. "Sure. I'll see you then."

I nod and follow my mom as I realize something: I have approximately three hours until my first ever date with Elle Carter.

*****

I grab the one collared shirt I packed for this weekend. Not that Elle is going to care, but my mom made a big stink about me getting ready for my date—which I firmly informed her is not a date—so I feel obligated to change into something other than a T-shirt.

I look at the time: six o'clock. An hour and a half to kill. I wander down the hallway toward the sound of voices. Our house isn't anywhere near the size of the Carters', meaning I easily heard Auntie Sharon and Auntie Lisa walk in our door about fifteen minutes ago.

I find them all settled around the table, a deck of cards being dealt out.

"Oliver, you're already ready?" my mom asks as Auntie Sharon sends a card flying her way like some sort of Vegas dealer.

"We're just going to go see Christmas lights, Mom. I don't think that calls for a tuxedo."

She studies my clothes with a critical eye. "I guess that'll do."

I'm glad my mom has decided I can acceptably dress myself after thirty years.

"Join us, Oliver," Auntie Sharon says as cards come sailing my way.

Knowing I might regret this, I ease onto the available chair.

"So," Auntie Lisa says, leaning toward me, "what's your take on Elle's new boyfriend?"

I guess we're getting right into it. "I'm very happy for her." I pick up my cards and shuffle them around mindlessly. "I assume he must be a good guy if Elle's dating him." Auntie Sharon snorts, and that regret I was worried about is creeping in.

Auntie Lisa plows on. "So you think he's real?"

"Of course the guy's not real." Auntie Sharon points to my cards. "We're playing Knock Out Whist. Seven rounds. Aces are high."

"I know your opinion, Sharon—that's why I'm asking for the boy's," her sister-in-law retorts.

Cards are being played in front of me at the speed of light, and I'm struggling to remember what the rules are. "Um, well, I assume he's real." I lay down a ten and immediately regret it when my mom gives me a comforting hand pat.

"You should've put down your queen," she whispers.

"So, you don't think there's any chance she's just pretending to have a boyfriend?" Auntie Sharon asks, scooping up the trick.

I forgot what card sharks these ladies were. "Um, should I?" I think back to what Noah said on the couch. Would Elle fake something like this? I toss out my queen this time, and my mom just shakes her head. I think I'm going to lose.

"Will you two leave well enough alone?" my mom says. "You're going to give Oliver a complex." She gives me a warm smile. Don't worry about what everyone's saying—"

Everyone?

"—you just go and have a nice time with Elle tonight, and be natural. Just let whatever happens, happen."

I'm not sure what she thinks is going to happen. We're going to watch a giant Christmas tree light up with a horde of neighborhood kids and families. Not exactly a risque outing.

I throw down a jack for the next round, which I know is a bad move, but at this point, I'm just trying to find an exit. A phone rings in someone's purse.

"Oh, that's me," Auntie Lisa says, digging through the oversized handbag she's slung on the back of the chair. She looks at the screen then announces to all of us that it's Tammy. "Hi, Tammy, I'm putting you on speakerphone. What's up?"

This seems the perfect time to disappear, but just as I'm about to sneak away, Tammy's voice comes out loud and clear. "If there's one thing Elle has given me, it's an assured spot in heaven. I'm telling you, ladies, getting that girl to do anything is like pulling teeth!"

Everyone's eyes shoot over to me, and I feel like a fish in a glass bowl.

"What's going on?" Auntie Lisa asks.

"I simply told her I thought it would be nice if she did herself up a little tonight. Put a curl in her hair, a touch of perfume behind the ears, a little lip-plumping gloss... You would think I had asked her to send me the moon and stars." Tammy lets out a dramatic sigh. "She's in the shower now, although I think it's mostly just to get away from the rest of us."

A vision of Elle in the shower with water dripping all over her flashes through my mind, and I have to physically brace myself against the table to keep my thoughts from going there.

"Anyway, she's only got about thirty minutes before the warm water runs out, so she can't stay in there forever. How's Oliver doing?"

Auntie Sharon wiggles her eyebrows at me. "He's right here. Anything else you want to tell him to build his confidence?"

Tammy's voice gets all sugary sweet. "Oliver! I didn't know you were listening."

I have a feeling if she were sitting here, she'd be staring daggers at her sisters-in-law.

"Elle is so grateful you're going to the tree lighting with her tonight, Oliver. I'm sure she'll be ready in no time."

I force a smile and set my cards down on the table. There's no way I can sit here and listen to the rest of this conversation. "Great, well, I just remembered an email I need to send out for work, so I'll leave you ladies to chat." I push back from the table. "I'll see Elle at seven-thirty," I call into the phone before spinning on my heel.

I'm starting to see how Elle might have been driven to invent a fake boyfriend.

*****

You'd think walking back over to my neighbor's house—the same house I've been hanging out at all afternoon—would be rather stress-free. But the minute I turn up the Carters' driveway, I am hit with a wall of nerves that makes me wonder if I need to sit down for a second.

What is my deal? This is just Elle. Sure, I've had a low-grade crush on her for basically forever, but that can't be enough to justify the sweat beading up on my palms. Maybe I wore too many layers?

I look at the pair of jeans and thin windbreaker. Considering it's about thirty degrees out, this isn't exactly over the top.

I inhale a few times before continuing my walk, my shoes crunching on the few patches of snow that weren't scraped free. Before I can even get to the porch, though, the oversized oak door is thrown open, and a chorus of voices greets me.

"Oliver! You're here!"

"Someone go get Elle!"

"Come in!"

"He's not coming in. He's leaving with Elle."

I'm clamping my teeth so hard my fillings must all be concerned for their lives.

"What's going on?"

I look past the horde of aunties and smirking brothers to see Elle standing at the foot of the stairs, one hand on her hip. She's traded those black leggings for an equally flattering pair of jeans that hug her hourglass figure spot on. A coat is thrown over one arm, and a gargantuan black-and-white scarf is draped about her neck, just screaming for someone to cuddle up with her by a roaring fire.

She must have done something to her hair, because it's loose around her face now. The silky brown strands aren't curly, but they're also not straight. They're somewhere in that middle, wavy ground that makes you wonder if it just dried like that or if she did it on purpose.

My eyes land on her face, and she's got one of those thin eyebrows cocked at me. How long have I been gaping?

"Hi, Elle. You...you look nice." Understatement of the year. She looks gorgeous, and a small part of me wonders if it's for me or just because her mom told her to dress up.

Everyone is still watching from the doorway, and most of the ladies have sappy smiles on their faces. I feel like I'm picking up my prom date. Where's our matching corsage and boutonniere? "You ready to go?" Time to get things moving.

She nods and elbows her way to the door. "Goodbye, everybody," she calls over her shoulder, sending one last sharp gaze to her mom. "I hope you ladies all have fun doing your *thing*."

"We will." Tammy's hands are clutched under her chin. "Now don't rush back or anything!"

I'm trying not to laugh as I follow Elle down the path to my SUV. I can see a tinge of pink in her cheeks, and I figure it's better to keep my mouth shut.

As we settle in, a wave of a warm vanilla scent hits me, and I'm suddenly sent to Memory Lane of an adolescent Oliver who used to inhale his mom's baking vanilla because it reminded him of the body spray Elle always wore. I'm surprised I never asphyxiated myself.

I give Elle a side glance as she runs her hands down her jeans, noting the berry red she's painted her nails. It reminds me of the red underwear that came flying out of her bag yesterday morning, and suddenly, I'm hit with how close our seats are situated. Why does this car feel so small?

I do my best to remember the steps of driving. Insert my key. Turn it to the right. Put my car in drive.

Silence hangs heavy between us.

I start cracking my knuckles at the first red light before I recall it's one of Elle's pet peeves. The quiet is killing me. I need to say something.

My hands go to the radio dial, an easy solution. "What do you want to listen to? Are you still a country guru?" Elle spent half her high school years hooked on Garth Brooks and LeAnn Rimes and the other half trying to convince the rest of us to listen to them too.

A little smile toys on her face. "I'm surprised you remember that."

Because I have clearly lost all ability to think before I talk around this woman, I blurt out, "I remember everything about you."

And then there's this Guinness-Book-of-World-Records-worthy awkward moment where we both stare at each other. Don't mind me, Elle, just the boy next door who apparently makes it his life goal to say embarrassing things in your presence.

She blinks, and the moment is broken. My head swivels back to look at the road, and she starts messing with the radio buttons. "I do love country still," she says as she finds a station playing enough twang to fill the entire state of Texas.

"I haven't heard this one in forever," Elle cries, cranking up the volume so high I worry about my speakers holding strong.

"Is it famous?" I ask.

Her mouth drops. "Oliver Moore, you'd better be kidding me. This is one of the greatest female country songs ever."

I scrunch up my face like I'm listening, but mostly, I'm just focused on the cute little lines between her eyebrows. "Hmm, I don't think I recognize it."

She purses her lips. "Really? If my memory is right, we listened to this song every morning during carpool my freshman year because it was on that CD mix Noah's girlfriend made for him. I swear he played it on repeat for six months straight."

I can't hold back my smile now. I do remember this song. And I do remember threatening to break the dumb CD just so Noah would stop playing it. "Maybe that rings a little bell."

Instead of answering, she starts singing, and I decide blown-out speakers are a small price to pay to hear her voice next to me. It's low and melodic, not a sound that would make a box hit or anything, but just smooth and comfortable. Like spreading butter on a warm piece of bread.

"*I hope you dance...*"

She looks at me and waves her hand in the air as if leading a choir. When I don't join in singing, she lowers her eyebrows and starts waving faster. I laugh and finally sing the one line that keeps repeating itself.

"*I hope you dance...*" I sing, my deeper voice playing well with hers.

The song ends just as I pull into the parking lot, and I've decided I'm converted to country music for life.

I peer through the window at the town center in front of us. There are surprisingly few people walking around considering this used to be one of the most well-attended city events every year.

"There doesn't seem to be very many people here," Elle says, voicing my own thoughts.

I open my door, and the cold night air seeps into my skin. "Let's go check it out."

We make our way to the small group of people, and I tap the shoulder of an older man. "Hi, is the tree lighting still going on tonight?"

He turns and gives me a nod. "It is. They're having some electrical issues, though, so they pushed it back a half an hour."

"Got it. Thank you." I walk back to Elle who is standing by the twenty-foot Christmas tree in the center of the square. "Good news and bad news. The tree lighting is still going on, but it's going to be a half-hour late." I glance at my watch. "So, we have about forty-five minutes to kill."

Elle's face falls a little. "Really?"

Even though I know this isn't a date, I feel an internal responsibility to make sure Elle has a good time. "Is there something you want to do in the meantime?" I look around. There's a large park connected to the town center. Most of it is covered in a thin layer of snow, but someone had the goodwill to blow it off of the basketball court. "Do you still remember how to shoot a basket?" I eye the boots she has on, wanting to retract my question. Of course she doesn't want to shoot baskets right now. It's freezing cold and dark.

She rolls her eyes as her gaze lands on the court. "Please, Moore. Don't act like you don't remember that time I smoked you in Horse. If I recall correctly, you've never challenged me since." That little grin is on her face again. "You're too scared."

I slip my keys out of my pocket, my mind going back to the game she's talking about. I remember it all too well— and definitely not because I lost. Because that day was the first time I wondered what it would be like to kiss Elle. She'd made this bank shot she'd been attempting the entire game and had surprised me by jumping in my arms in celebration. I'd just turned fifteen, and every teenage hormone was raging with that second's worth of body contact.

Yeah, I never challenged her to a basketball game again after that. But it had nothing to do with the fact that she'd won. "Let's see if history repeats itself. I have a ball in the back of my car."

Chapter 7 - Elle

If you'd told me two days ago that I'd be playing a game of Horse on a dimly lit city basketball court with Oliver Moore, I would've said you were dreaming.

And yet, here I am.

I dribble the ball, the tips of my fingers feeling more numb with every bounce. Lining up my elbow, I take the same shot I've been attempting for the last ten minutes, cursing under my breath when it bounces off the rim.

"You almost made it that time," Oliver says as he retrieves my ball. "I mean, at this level, you'd for sure make the high school's freshman team."

I scoop up a hunk of snow and launch it at his face. Unfortunately, it only hits his shoulder, but I feel better seeing the white splatter on his jacket.

He grins and dribbles a few times. "All right, bank shot, from behind the stick." He points his sneaker at a stray branch by his feet. He shoots, and the ball slips through the net way too easily.

I groan as it bounces back to him. "You have an unfair advantage. I didn't know we'd be playing basketball, or I wouldn't have worn snow boots." It's partially true. These things are dragging me down. But it could also be that I haven't shot a basket in five years.

"I'm just disappointed you didn't wear heels or something. Then I'd really have an edge—and a show." He wiggles his eyebrows before stretching out his arm with the ball.

I stomp toward him and grab it from his hands. Do I notice how warm his fingers feel? Yes. Would I love nothing more than to have him wrap me up in a body-warming bear hug? Maybe.

Purely from a survival aspect, though. Cold kills.

I'm getting into my shooting stance when I feel a strong arm around my waist, pulling me to the side.

"Over here, missy. Don't try cheating."

I look down and realize the stick is two feet to my right, so I step over, acutely aware of his hand resting on my hip a split-second longer than necessary.

His dark eyes are almost black in the dim light, and he's not smiling, but there's a happy look on his face. Like he's perfectly content to be playing basketball with me on this freezing night instead of hanging out with his guy friends, watching football. One lock of his unruly hair has fallen across his forehead, giving him that boyish look from our childhood.

How much about this man has changed over the years? What about him and his life do I not know? I have this sudden urge to learn everything about him.

I look at the ball in my hand, my fingers barely feeling the rubber edges under them. "How's business going these days?" I can see the way his eyebrows rise out of the corner of my eye.

"You want to hear about my work?"

I quickly throw the ball in the air, mostly to kill the weird tension between us. It bounces off the backboard. Dang it. "Yeah, I haven't seen you in, I don't know, three or four years now? Back then, your company was just getting off the ground. It sounds like you're established now."

He dribbles, and for the first time, I realize the only thing he's wearing out here is a light windbreaker. Typical. When we were kids, he used to insist on wearing shorts year-round, no matter what his mom said.

"It's going well. A lot better than I ever hoped." He plants his feet like he's about to shoot but just holds the ball in his hands. "I initially had a few big projects that helped spread the word, but I like to think the quality of our work speaks for itself."

"You always were good at paying attention to details," I say just as he throws the ball up. If I'm not mistaken, his arm seems to wobble at the last second, and the shot ricochets off the rim.

"Attention to detail?"

I shrug and watch the ball roll across the court. "Yeah, I mean, don't get a complex about it or anything, but you were more aware than at least my brothers ever were."

He folds his arms. "I'm gonna need more info than that."

I can feel my cheeks heating up. I hadn't meant to make a big deal of it. "I don't know, like in that biology class we took together. I'm pretty sure you were the only one that actually followed through and did the whole PowerPoint presentation like the teacher asked. The rest of us just made some crappy posters." I bend down and grab the basketball that's stopped at my feet. "Or the fact that you always thanked my mom every time you came over to eat. My brothers just shoveled in whatever she put in front of them, but you always took the time to tell her how delicious her food was. She always made her best meals when she knew you were coming over." That was half the reason Noah invited Oliver over for dinner so often. "Or even just the fact that you remember country music is my favorite. I doubt anybody else in my family would know that."

He grins and takes a step toward me. "Elle, I'm sure everyone on the block knows country is your favorite the way you blared it twenty-four seven."

"Someone had to drown out the nonstop sound of ESPN." He's just staring at me now, and I feel like a bug under a microscope.

"Well, thank you, I guess. I never thought you were paying any attention to me."

My body is heating up like a furnace despite the cold. I would consider taking off my jacket if it wouldn't be totally weird. We are basically in a field of snow. "I mean, it's not like I was paying you *special* attention or anything. Those were just things I happened to notice. Occasionally. You know, when the opportunity arose, and I couldn't help...noticing them. I wasn't trying to." *Shut up, Elle.*

He's biting his lip like he's holding back a laugh. "Has anyone ever told you you're really good at keeping a guy's ego in check?"

He takes another step toward me, and I'm tracking him like a hunter. Two more steps and he'll be right by my side. "That sounded harsher than I meant. Ignore me. I just mean, I'm not surprised at your company's success." I dribble. We need to get back to basketball. That's safe. "You deserve it." Without glancing at the basket, I chuck the ball up, not even caring what happens to it until I hear the telltale swoosh.

My eyes shoot up to the hoop. The net is still moving, and the ball is bouncing right underneath it. "Did I make that? Did I make one?" I jump in the air, and my arms instinctively go out for a victory hug. It's only at the last second that I remember who's standing in front of me and that hugging isn't our status quo.

Oliver's eyes are wide, his hands raised just slightly as if he's about to ward off an attack from a bear.

Oh my gosh, what does this look like to him?

I drop one arm and lift the other higher as if I'm waiting for him to give me a high five. Like, obviously, why would I attempt a hug? Why would anyone ever want a hug from those broad shoulders and chiseled muscles? No, thank you. I am strictly a palm-smacking, no-other-body-parts-touching kind of girl. Friend-zone-only celebrations.

I swallow, telling myself I'm giving him two seconds to return this high five before I drop my hand.

Almost in slow motion, he lifts his palm to mine. Instead of giving it a hard slap, though, he grabs my hand and interlocks our fingers, lifting our arms in a victory sign. "Good job," he finally says, his voice lower than before. His eyes are burning a hole in mine with their penetrating stare, as if he's searching my soul for an answer to something.

My mouth is dry, and I swallow, but apparently, the Sahara Desert has taken up residence in my body, and it does nothing to help.

Oliver takes another step toward me, bringing our hands down. There's less than a foot of space between us, and I can smell cologne on him. It's faint, but the fresh, clean scent gives me a slightly heady feeling. I command my eyes to stick to his forehead, but they hitchhike their way down to his mouth where his lips are parted softly.

He's going to kiss me.

Oliver Moore is going to kiss me.

I've spent almost fifteen years trying to put as much space and platonic aura between us as possible, and at this moment, I can't think of a single thing I want more in this world than his lips on mine. I hold my breath, my eyelids already half closing as he leans in.

"And here I was, thinking I'd have to cradle your bruised ego all the way home."

His voice is low and intimate, and it takes me a second to realize he's not whispering terms of endearment in my ear but a jab at my basketball skills.

It's like stepping into the shower and accidentally turning the water to cold instead of warm. My eyes snap open, and I take a sharp breath of the frigid air, which just adds to the dryness of my lungs and starts a coughing fit an asthmatic could claim.

Oliver jumps behind me and pounds my back. "Elle? Are you okay?"

I can hear his voice between hacks, but there's little I can do at this point until the coughing stops. I step back, waving him off.

He ignores my gestures and stays close, mimicking my hunched-over position, hands on his knees. "You're okay. Slow, deep breaths," he says, his low voice surprisingly soothing given the fact that I'm irritated as heck at him.

I follow his words, trying to calm my wheezing. It's only after another minute of waffling back and forth between more coughs and deep breaths that I'm able to get control.

I stand, wiping the tears streaming down my face, wishing I could just as easily wipe the last three minutes from Oliver's memory. I know that moment is going to replay in my mind the entire night, like a nightmare that actually happened. Why would I think he was going to kiss me? Oliver doesn't feel that way about me, and even if he did, I have a boyfriend. He might be a completely fake boyfriend, but Oliver doesn't know that. "S-sorry about that," I say, my voice still a little raspy.

I feel a squeeze on my arm and realize it's Oliver's hand trying to steady me. "No problem," he says, his voice still that calm tone. "I forgot you get these coughing attacks. You want some water? I think I have some in my car."

I shake my head. "No, I'm fine now." He's unfortunately right. These coughing fits have been a common occurrence for me my entire life. I'd been tested for asthma, but they always came back negative. The doctors just told me I have a tendency to get dry airways—an issue enhanced by the winter air.

Oliver's hand still has a firm grip on my arm, as if he thinks I'm going to tip over at any second.

The sound of voices reaches us from the town center.

Oliver checks his watch. "It's eight-thirty. I bet they're lighting the tree." His eyes go up and down my body as if he's not sure I can make the thirty-yard walk. "Do you want to watch it or just go home?"

I roll my eyes, even though I'm kinda loving how concerned he is. There's something innately attractive about a knight in shining armor. Although, that information will go with me to my grave. "I'm fine, Oliver. Let's get over there."

He doesn't look convinced, but he shrugs and retrieves the basketball.

A minute later, we're standing on the edge of the crowd that's gathered to watch the tree lighting. There are significantly more people than forty-five minutes ago, but the tree is so big you can see it from any spot.

"Welcome, welcome, everyone!" A portly man wearing a festive red hat and Christmas sweater is speaking into a microphone at the front. I don't recognize him, but he must be the current mayor. He talks for a few minutes, thanking everyone for coming and giving the history of the tree lighting.

I can feel the chill of the night seeping into my limbs now that we're no longer moving around. Oliver stamps his feet next to me, and I wonder how he's faring in his light windbreaker.

"*Three...two...one...*"

I must've missed the start of the countdown, but I catch on just as everyone yells *Go!*

The dark tree in front of us lights up with thousands of white twinkly lights that feel a little like magic against the blackness of the night. Red bulbs are reflecting back the light, and the popsicle-stick ornaments that must have been supplied by some of the local schools give the whole thing a cozy look.

Someone picks up a chorus of "Oh, Christmas Tree," and soon, everyone is singing along.

I look around us. There's a smattering of families with small kids hanging on to their parent's legs, gazing in awe at the tree. There are older couples with arms comfortably linked and younger couples staring at each other as much as they are at the tree.

Where do Oliver and I fit in this mix?

He turns his head toward me. "If you look real close, you'll see there's a missing row of lights about midway up." He points about three feet above our heads. "We had a busted strand of lights, but we didn't realize it until they were already on there. I made the executive decision to go with it rather than unwind everything."

I lift my eyebrows. "You helped put the tree up?" Dimples are popping at me, and I conclude then and there that his smile is the most adorable one I've ever seen.

"I don't know if I'm offended or not by your surprise," he says, still leaning in close. "But yes, I'm an outstanding citizen and often help out with these town events. They need a strapping young man around to climb the ladders."

He winks, and I melt a little more. Why would I expect anything less of Oliver? I smile at him. "You did a great job despite the busted strand of lights. The tree looks magical."

He looks down at me, and that same expression from the basketball court—the one where it looks like he's trying to figure something out—is on his face. "I'm glad you like it." Then, as if it's the most everyday thing in the world, he links his arm through mine, pulling me close. Without saying another word, he begins singing with the crowd that has now moved on to "Silent Night."

A small part of me knows I should pull back, knows I should protest in honor of my boyfriend. (What is his name again? Matt?) But maybe, just this once, it's fine. I rest my head against his shoulder, the heat from his body filling my cheek.

At this moment, nothing feels more right.

Chapter 8 - Elle

You know those mornings after a big date? The kind where your roommates gather to break down every word that was said, every romantic gesture given, every squeal-worthy moment from the night before?

It's a whole different feeling when it's your mom interrogating you.

"You had to have done *something* other than look at a dumb tree," my mom says, re-wiping the same spot on the counter she's been polishing for the last five minutes. "It only takes, like, ten seconds to plug in Christmas lights."

I take another bite of cereal, wishing I could bury my face in the sugary concoction. Oliver and I stuck around at the tree lighting for half an hour or so, singing carols and just enjoying the ambiance before coming home.

It had been a mistake. My mom had interpreted every minute we were gone as one more minute working toward Oliver being her future son-in-law.

"I told you, Mom, they started the tree lighting late. And then when I got home, you guys were all playing games in the family room, so I just went upstairs to bed." I let out a dramatic yawn as evidence of my sleepiness. "That's it. We watched the tree light up, sang some songs with the neighborhood, then came home." My answer is true on the surface. Technically, that's all we did. Is there any need to bring up the somewhat flirtatious basketball game? My bizarre desire for him to kiss me? Our obvious connection while watching the tree lighting? The fact that I'd enjoyed every minute I spent with Oliver last night?

I shove another bite into my mouth. I'm weakening. I have to get back to my plan: continue talking up this boyfriend of mine—was his name James?—and spend as little time as possible with Oliver.

The timer on the oven dings, and my mom throws down her rag with a huff. "I literally set her up with a perfect romantic night, and the girl can't even manage to..."

I hum to tune out my mom's muttering.

"Good morning," Noah says, walking in with my two-year-old nephew in his arms. "Mmm, are those cinnamon rolls, Mom? We are going to need a couple of those each."

"Of course, my baby needs his nourishment," my mom says, scooping out hot rolls onto a plate.

"Mom, I'm a little old for you to be calling me baby," my brother says, settling his son onto a stool along the bar.

"I'm not talking about you. You can fend for yourself." My mom slides the plate in front of her grandson. "I'm talking about one of the cutest little boys in the entire world."

Noah looks at me and grins. "A word to the wise...if you ever want Mom to start ignoring you, give the woman some grandchildren. You'll be last week's news."

My mom swats him with a spatula but hands him a cinnamon roll too.

"Elle, can you help wrap presents this morning?" My mom slides a plate my way as well. "I've got a few bags from the community toy drive. They're all going to the shelter tomorrow."

I take the plate from her, a small part of me wishing I could say no, solely because a wrapping session is just another opportunity for her to question me about Oliver. "Sure," I say, breaking off a piece of cinnamon-saturated dough.

"I smell something good!"

Auntie Lisa's voice carries down the hallway followed by the slam of the front door. She comes around the corner, arms full of wrapping paper. "Cinnamon rolls! Gosh, I love the holidays, but they sure take a hit on my waistline." She pinches a piece from the pan. "Elle, how was your date last night? Any sparks fly?"

This is going to be a long morning. "It wasn't a date. I have a boyfriend, and Oliver and I are just friends."

She gives a meaningful look to my mom. "Okaaay...but in my day, when a man took a woman to a romantic event like a tree lighting on a snowy night, usually a little something-something happened before—"

"There are children present," Noah says, covering the ears of his child that definitely has no idea what Auntie Lisa is talking about.

I need to fill my life with more children—as protection.

My aunt and brother start discussing what time my cousins are coming in today while I rinse out my bowl. "Okay, Mom," I say, shutting the dishwasher with my hip, "what do you need from me?"

"There are a couple bags of toys in my bedroom," she says, digging through her purse on the counter. "I have a list here with all the names of what's for who." She waves a folded sheet in the air. "Ah-ha, here it is. Can you bring them down, and I'll go get the scissors and tape? We'll do it at the dining room table." She taps her sister-in-law on the shoulder as she walks out of the kitchen. "Go set up at the table. Elle's going to grab the toys."

Fifteen minutes later, we have a full wrapping station set up that any department store would be proud of. My mom is creating the labels, my aunt and I are in charge of wrapping, and Autumn, who got suckered into helping as soon as she came downstairs, is in charge of bows.

"So, tell us more about this boyfriend of yours," my mom says, literally one present into our operation. "You have to know I'm still shocked since I've never heard anything about the man until now."

I measure out a sheet of snowman wrapping paper for a Barbie set. "Mom, have you seen the pestering I've gotten since I've been home? Of course I'm not going to tell you when I'm dating someone. That's all I would hear about from then on."

"You know your mother just wants what's best for you," Auntie Lisa says as she grabs a roll of Christmas tree paper. "All moms do. It's our job. Now, what does this man do for a living? Will he be a good provider?"

And that's how I find myself spending the next fifteen minutes creating a fake persona for the made-up man I'm not dating. By the time Autumn asks what his hobbies are, I'm not even sure if I'm keeping my facts straight.

"How's the wrapping coming?" Rhett leans over my mom's shoulder, eyeing the Lego Batman set she's holding. "I sure hope that one's for Brett and not me. You know I prefer Superman."

My mom sticks a bow on his forehead. "These are toys for the local shelter. Sit down, and you can help."

Rhett leaves the bow on his face and finds a free seat. He starts unraveling a spool of crimped ribbon that I doubt he even knows how to use. "So," he says, a glint in his eye that makes me nervous, "Brett and I were just talking about the Christmas shopping we have left, and I was wondering what you got your dear boyfriend this year, Elle. It must be something good since you two aren't even together for the holidays."

I grit my teeth and slice through the paper with more force than necessary. "We agreed not to get each other anything this year." I don't know if I can come up with a good Christmas present for an attractive man in his early thirties, who is a business manager and likes golf and Italian food, on the spot. For some reason, that was the persona I came up with for him.

"Did you get anything for Oliver?" my mom cuts in.

I scrunch my nose. "Why would I get something for Oliver? We're not exactly the gift-exchanging kind of friends."

My mom sends me an annoyed look. "What do you mean? Oliver and you always went to each other's birthday parties growing up. You've been giving each other gifts since you were babies."

Why is it so hard to reason with your own mother? "Yes, Mom, back in elementary school."

"I beg to differ," Rhett says, still twirling the same spool of ribbon and doing zero work. "Don't you remember that promise ring he gave you for your sixteenth birthday? The one you kept for years?"

Ugh. Leave it to my brother to remember all the obscure, embarrassing details of my life. I make the executive decision to pretend like I don't know what he's talking about. "What ring?"

He leans back in his chair, a little grin playing across his face. "Don't play coy with me. That silver one with a little purple jewel that you kept in your jewelry box."

It was actually a pink jewel, and I'm suddenly very engrossed in my wrapping job. "Are you sure you're not thinking of a ring you gave *your* girlfriend?"

He pushes back from the table, and I immediately know I've made a mistake. "I guarantee you still have it. I'm going to go find it."

I scramble to my feet, but I'm caught up in a web of paper and tape. "Rhett, don't you dare!" He's already gone, though, and I'm left wracking my brain, trying to remember if I ever did get rid of that ring.

The ring was in no way a promise ring, despite what Rhett says. And it had been my fifteenth birthday, not my sixteenth. But it was true...Oliver did give it to me.

My family had gone to a bowling alley for my birthday. All my aunts, uncles, cousins, and of course Oliver and his mom were there. Because despite what a genetics test would tell us, they are family. Halfway through the evening, I went to the bathroom and came out to see Oliver leaning against one of those coin toy dispensers—the ones where you put your quarter in, and a little plastic-enclosed prize comes out when you twist the knob.

He wished me a happy birthday and said he felt bad he'd forgotten to get me a present. I'd brushed him off, spending most of the conversation staring at my shoes because I had a hard time looking him in the eyes those days without blushing. Somehow, Oliver ended up dropping a few quarters in one of the dispensers, with the intention of getting me a present. The first one had come out with a toy soldier, and the second had been an eraser. I spent most of the time being mesmerized by those adorable dimples that half the girls in my grade were in love with. I almost missed it when he insisted the third time was a charm. Seconds later, out shot a container with a silver ring housing a light-pink jewel in the middle. It was one of those cheap metal ones where you could tighten it simply by pushing on the prongs. But the way he presented it to me, you would've thought it held a rare diamond.

It was one of the few times I remember relaxing in his presence. Whether it was the ridiculousness of the gift or the fact that it was my birthday and I was feeling bold, I let go of my reserved tendencies and took the ring from him, laughing.

When I got home that night, I couldn't decide what to do with it. A small part of me thought I should toss it. It really had no monetary value, and it was just a joke. But instead, I found myself placing it in the jewelry box where I kept all my special things. Things I wanted to treasure and didn't want anyone else to see.

I shake my head. Apparently, I hadn't been as good at keeping that box as hidden as I thought.

Footsteps pound down the stairs, and a second later, Rhett walks in holding the ring high above his head. "Told ya you never got rid of this thing."

The sound of the front door slamming followed by an all-too-familiar voice shoots my heart rate up to dangerous territory.

Oliver.

Next thing I know, he, Brett, and my cousin Logan are walking into the room.

"What have you three been doing?" Auntie Lisa asks as they come around the corner.

"Dad asked me to fix the Christmas lights on the house," Logan says, lifting up an orange extension cord in his hands. "Brett and Oliver wanted a lesson in lighting, so I let them tag along."

Brett elbows him, and Oliver grabs the cord from his hands. "Logan tried to soup up your Christmas lights," Oliver says. "He tripped the breaker and needed our help fixing it before Uncle Marlo found out."

Logan's face turns a bright red, but he shrugs good-naturedly. "Potato, po-ta-to. Are there any cookies left, Auntie Tammy?"

My mom points to the giant Tupperware on the counter. "Go fill up. You boys are all too skinny."

I shake my head. My mom's dying words will be that everyone is too skinny.

"Hey, Oliver," Rhett says, his eyes landing on me. "Guess what we found in Elle's sacred box of memories today."

I can feel my face heating up, and I'm sure I'm giving Logan's blush a run for its money. I know deep—very deep—down inside of me I love my little brother, but at the present moment, I could literally kill him.

Oliver is staring at the ring in Rhett's hand, his eyebrows knit together. I'm sure he has no idea what it is. I don't even know why the heck I've kept the thing so long. It's nothing. A stupid ring from a stupid coin dispenser. I'd rather have my underwear spilled all over the driveway again than be sitting here, listening to this.

"What is that?" Oliver asks, stepping toward Rhett.

"You don't remember the promise ring you gave Elle back in high school?" Rhett is enjoying this way too much.

"It's not a promise ring," I mutter, my face now pressed into my hands.

Now Brett is getting into the mix. "Hey, I remember that thing. We found it in Elle's jewelry box, and Mom made us put it back."

That's it. I can't take it anymore. I stand up and snatch the ring from Rhett's hand. Before I can stomp upstairs and wallow in a good cry and probably a phone call to Sophie, Oliver grabs my hand.

If it had been anyone else, I would've jerked my fingers free. But his touch, while strong, is soft, almost like he's cradling a newborn kitten. "Can I see it?" he asks, his voice low, as if the question is for me only.

I open up my fist, the ring seeming tiny in the center of my palm. His hand grazes mine for a split-second before taking the ring from me, holding it up to his face. As tiny as it looked in my hand, it's dwarfed by his thick fingers. He slides it onto his pinky, not even able to get it past the first knuckle.

"I do remember this," he says, looking up at me. His voice is still quiet, although I know everyone in the room is eavesdropping with gusto the FBI would be proud of. "I gave it to you on your fifteenth birthday at the bowling alley."

At least someone remembers it was my fifteenth. I nod, chewing on the corner of my lip.

As he studies the ring, I study him. He's wearing gray corduroys and a flannel shirt that gives him a strange combination of a boy-next-door look along with a rugged, about-to-go-chop-down-a-tree kind of look. My eyes land on his arms for a second, the ones that had been linked through mine just last night. The flush of heat that had collected on my face a moment ago is now rendezvousing throughout my whole body.

He offers the ring back to me. "I can't believe you've kept it all these years," he says, but it's not said in a teasing way, like my brothers' words. It's said almost with a hint of awe, like he's honored.

I swallow and grab the ring, twirling it between my fingers. "Well, you know, it's rude to get rid of a gift and all that, isn't it?" I'm stuttering a little, but it's hard to think straight when he's staring at me like it's Sunday morning and I'm a brunch buffet.

"Yeah, of course." His voice is soft again, and time seems to stand still between the two of us. It's almost like he's waiting for me to tell him the truth. To tell him I kept the ring because it reminded me of him. It reminded me of his goodness and how much he cared about people. How he could make the smallest gesture feel like the biggest thing in the world. To tell him that if things had been different, if we hadn't been caught in this hoopla of family dynamics, it might've been different between us.

But then I hear someone cough behind me, and the moment breaks.

I forget we are surrounded by one of the world's nosiest, most busybody families in the world.

I look at the table to see all eyes on us. My mom is wiping one eye with her sleeve, and Auntie Lisa has her phone out, recording everything.

For the love.

"Anyway, there's nothing like good old childhood memories," I say in a loud voice as I step back. Nothing going on over here. No sparks flying through the air, no meaningful glances, no spine-tingling emotions rushing through my body. I clap my hands. "So, where are we with the present wrapping?"

I settle in my chair, trying to get back into the flow. Although, it is a little difficult, knowing Oliver is still about two feet behind me. What happened to all my resolve I showed up with twenty-four hours ago? What happened to the plan of keeping my emotions in check? Of keeping the only man who could turn all my insides into applesauce at arm's length?

I glance over my shoulder to see him still staring at me. He steps close and squats down, his elbows resting on the table. "What are you working on here?"

Gosh, he smells good. Why does he have to smell so good? My breathing feels irregular, and my palms are sweating. "Just wrapping up some toys for the homeless shelter. Want to help?" Why did I invite him to help me?

"Of course." He pulls a chair close to me. "What can I do?"

A few non-family-friendly suggestions come to mind, but thanks to my boss, I've had a lot of practice ignoring bad ideas. "Why don't you help tape?" I say, doing my best to not dwell on whether or not his voice always sounds that rumbly and tension-filled.

"Have you recovered from our basketball game yesterday?" he asks a moment later, ripping off a piece of tape and handing it to me.

"Recovered? I'm pretty sure I didn't even break a sweat." I can see him grinning from the corner of my eye. "To be honest, I wasn't even trying that hard. I know your ego was bruised last time I beat you, and I didn't want history to repeat itself." The piece of tape gets stuck on my thumb, and I wiggle my hand in the air, trying to free it while my other hand holds the wrapping paper edges down.

Without pause, his hands come on either side of mine, holding the cut pieces of paper together so I can get the tape off my finger. "I'm beginning to think you staged that whole coughing fit just to get out of the competition."

I am having a hard time acting normal now that his body is completely pressed against mine. The gesture seems innocent on the outside, but it feels like a deliberate attack on my heartbeat's functionality. I grab the tape on my thumb, lobbing it at the wrapping paper in hopes that he'll back away, and I can breathe again.

Instead of removing his hands, though, he almost leans in closer, forcing me to take a gasping breath that isn't embarrassing at all or anything.

"So, you admit it?"

I'm not sure if he's referring to my struggle to get oxygen into my body or something else. "Admit what?"

"That you purposely forfeited our game of Horse last night."

Is that what we're talking about? It seems like an awfully bland topic, given the close proximity of our bodies. Not to mention the fact that I don't think I've ever studied his lips this close up before. Wait. What am I doing staring at his lips? "Uh, no. D-definitely not." Oh my gosh, now I'm stuttering. "I'll take you on any time."

His eyes bore into mine, that little grin and those darn dimples seductively teasing every feminine hormone in my body.

"I'd meet you anywhere you want, Elle."

A deaf man could've heard the sensual tension in that comment.

"Do you think he's going to kiss her?"

My auntie's whisper zips me back to the present like Dorothy being whipped home to Kansas. Both Oliver and I turn our heads to see the rest of the table watching our interaction.

In slow motion, he retracts his arms, pulling himself a very polite two feet away from me and my raging ovaries. Instead of sitting back in his chair, though, he stands. "You know, I should be going," he says, his voice loud enough for everyone to hear. "I actually just came over because my mom wanted me to confirm that we're all still caroling tonight."

I hold back a groan. I forgot the Carter Christmas tradition of caroling at the retirement villa every Christmas Eve Eve. It was a nice gesture when we were all cute little five-years-olds, singing "Here Comes Santa Claus," but we started putting up some serious protests during my high school years. If it wasn't for my mother's iron will, the tradition would've died out long ago.

"Of course," my mom says. "Tell your mom we'll leave at seven."

Oliver heads off, and I let out a slow breath of air.

Only forty-eight hours left until I'm done with this trip. I can stay strong for that long.

The question is, do I still want to?

Chapter 9 - Oliver

A head case. Elle has officially turned me into a head case the last two days.

A small part of me knows I'll always carry a flame for her. But I've always assumed that flame would eventually shrink until it's nothing but a dying birthday-cake candle.

In the last two days, though, that flame has turned into a roaring bonfire. The kind you make from burning a year's worth of homework, neighborhood Christmas trees, and everything else potentially flammable in the universe— which isn't okay, considering I'm not sure where Elle stands.

Sure, there were some flirtatious vibes going on last night, but they were intermixed with moments when Elle would pull back, as if she realized we were crossing into uncharted territory.

And then there's this mysterious boyfriend. Is he even real? I mean, other than the phone call yesterday, I've seen no evidence that she's in a committed relationship. I swear, if we hadn't been surrounded by her overzealous family today, nothing would've stopped me from leaning forward and kissing her senseless after seeing that ring. Because there's no denying it's a kiss I've dreamed about for years.

"I'm headed over to the Carters'! Can you feed Buzz on your way out?" My mom's voice snaps me out of my daydream.

"Yeah," I call back. I jump off the bed and grab my shoes in the corner. I'm normally a straight-laced guy. A rule follower and a line toer. But maybe it's time to break that streak. Maybe it's time to push Elle a little.

I think back to that dazed look on her face, the way she chewed her bottom lip—a nervous tick she's had since she was little. Maybe that flame of ours doesn't need to be put out. Maybe it just needs a little more fuel.

*****

Just as I'm walking up the Carters' driveway, I hear a car pull up to the curb. I turn to see a guy in a black snow jacket, carrying a vase of...are those flowers?

He stops when he sees me, the snow crunching under his shoes. "Hi, I have a delivery for a..." He eyes the slip of paper attached to the red roses. "Elle Carter?"

A chill comes over my body. Red roses? That can only be from one person. I reach out for the vase. "Yep, you've got the right place."

He hands the glass to me. "Awesome. Have a good day."

I nod, but my mind is busy going a million miles a second. Elle really does have a boyfriend. There really is someone else in her life. The chill has dissolved into a dull pit in my stomach. I can't infringe on something like that.

Eyeing the little white envelope, I have an unmistakable urge to slide out the card and read exactly what this dude has written to her.

But instead, I walk toward the door. I'm not that kind of guy.

I slip off my shoes and follow the sound of voices to the back of the house. As I step into the family room, a flurry of motion greets my eyes. My mom and the aunties are on the couch, discussing who knows what. The men are all in the kitchen, devouring whatever concoction Tammy has baked for them. And then there's Elle and Autumn, sitting at the table, coloring with the two little boys. Christmas music is playing in the background, and a small fire is going in the fireplace.

Even in its chaos, it looks perfect. This family, these bonds are ones I know I want to have forever. I just wish Elle felt the same way about me.

"Oliver? Oh my gosh, did you bring Elle flowers?" Auntie Carol's voice carries across the room with a deafening shrill. All at once, the group goes silent, everyone turning to look at me.

My mom is the first to react. "Oh, honey, roses? That is so sweet of you!"

She jumps up, quickly followed by Tammy. Both the ladies charge forward, and I'm not sure whether it's for me or the flowers.

"No." I lift the vase high, out of their painted fingernails' reach. "I didn't. These are for Elle—but they're not from me." Despite the avalanche of questions coming at me, my eyes zero in on her at the table. Unlike everyone else, she's not looking at the flowers but at me.

"Who are they from then?" someone calls out.

As if suddenly realizing there is a horde of family members about to stampede her boyfriend's gift, Elle shoots to her feet and comes toward me. "They must be from..." Her voice dies, and she's chewing her bottom lip as she takes the vase. "From Brad, of course."

"Brad?" One of the twins leans over her shoulder and, with lightning speed, grabs the white card. Apparently, he doesn't have the same scruples about reading other people's notes like me. "I thought you said his name was Danny."

She snatches the card out of his hands but not before he reads out loud, "See, it says right here: *Love and miss you, Danny.*"

Elle's face is beet red, and she's heedlessly crumbling the card in her fingers. "Brad is h-his middle name. That's what most of his friends call him."

Brett's eyes are still narrowed. "Danny Brad?"

I have to agree it is a little odd sounding.

"Yes, isn't it nice?" Her words sound about as convincing as nothing. "I'm going to go put these in my room and grab my jacket for caroling."

At the word *caroling*, everybody seems to unfreeze. "Yes," Tammy says, clapping her hands, "everyone make sure you have shoes and a coat. We're leaving in five minutes for the retirement villa."

There's a flurry of activity around me, but my mind is still focused on Elle scurrying up the stairs.

"Oliver, dear," Tammy's hand is on my arm. "Do you mind driving? I'm not sure if we'll have enough cars." Her eyes shift from me to the now-empty staircase. "If you don't mind taking Elle, that would be nice. I think she needs some separation from her brothers."

I almost say that I think she needs some separation from the whole family, but I manage to hold it in and nod. "Sure, I can do that."

She gives me a pat on my arm and walks away.

*****

"...*we wish you a Merry Christmas and a happy new year!*"

Logan gives the bells he's holding an extra-long jingle as we finish the song. The crowd of elderly listeners offers us a spattering of applause and smiles, which is more than we can ask for, given our talent level. I think Brett and Rhett's hilarious antics during the performance made up for our lack of musical talent.

I look on the other side of the group to see Elle adjusting the reindeer antlers on her head. She's the only one in the world that can make a pair of plastic antlers look adorable.

As her mom requested, we drove here together. Although, I don't think it was the peaceful, romantic ride Tammy was envisioning. Somehow, her twin brothers and Logan ended up in the backseat, and we spent the majority of the time discussing why college football was more entertaining than the NFL. What I wouldn't give to go back to that tree lighting where it was just me and her.

Tammy begins ushering our group out of the room. "All right, we're going to sing in the cafeteria and then finish in the library."

There is an expected amount of mumbling and shuffling as everyone follows our queen bee back into the hallway. I'm sure our caroling brings a measure of joy, but sometimes I think these people would appreciate it more if we just sat and chatted with them. As we're walking down the hallway, I see a room with puzzles, board games, and people scattered at different tables. Before I can second-guess myself, I slide over to Elle and hook her by the elbow.

She gives a little yelp, but I place one finger to my lips. Hoping no one notices, I yank her into the doorway of the room I'm inspecting.

"What are we doing?" she asks, putting up little resistance.

"I don't know, I just thought it'd be fun to chat with some of these people for a bit. It's not like the group needs our voices." That is actually a lie. Elle is one of the better singers, and her strong alto will be sorely missed.

Her eyes rove around the room before coming back to me. "Okay," she says with a shrug.

An older man doing a puzzle looks up and waves us over. "You two any good at these?"

I smile and nod to Elle. "I can't say I'm an expert, but this girl is one of the smartest people I know. Plus, she's an accountant, so she's got to be good at puzzles."

Elle lifts an eyebrow. "One of the smartest people you know?"

I tilt my head. "Well, yeah. You're the one that zipped through high school with straight As like it was nothing. And don't even pretend you didn't have a full academic ride all through college."

Her cheeks are tinged that pink color I love a little too much. "Thanks, I guess. I never thought I was any smarter than anyone else."

I look at the puzzle. "I guess we'll see if my bragging about you is right in a few minutes."

Her lips spread into a wide smile, every laugh line on her face visible. "Lucky for me I actually am good at puzzles."

We settle in at the man's table, and in about fifteen minutes, we've learned the highlights of his life. His name is Bill, and he is a retired mail carrier who has three kids and eight grandchildren. His wife lived here at the villa with him until two years ago when she passed away from cancer.

We make the appropriate hums and ahs during his stories until we all eventually lapse into a comfortable silence. There's Christmas music playing in the background and a pleasant scent of pine that must be coming from the tiny Christmas tree on the far side of the room. It's like a little corner of Christmas heaven, for just us.

"So, speaking of accounting, you never finished telling me about work," I say to Elle, pushing a few pieces around with my finger. "Do you think you'll stick it out with your company long-term? Or is it just a stepping stone?"

She studies the two pieces in her hands. "I don't know. When I started, I thought I was in it for the long haul. You know, holding strong until I make partner." She places one of her pieces in an open slot, and it fits perfectly.

I shake my head. She has to be on her sixth or seventh piece, and I still have yet to find one.

"But I'm starting to wonder if it's not the right path for me. I really hate my boss, and the long hours are wearing on me."

My internal Hulk rumbles at the thought of her working for anyone that doesn't appreciate her. If there is one thing I know, it's that when Elle puts her mind to something, she goes full throttle. Her boss is lucky to have her.

"Not that I'm saying I have all the answers," Bill says, not even looking up from the piece he's examining, "but I do have eighty-seven years of life experience under my belt." He reaches out and nestles his piece in an open spot.

I am, apparently, the weak link of this group.

"If there's one thing I know," he continues, "it's that it is not worth it to work for a person or company you dislike. Before I became a mail carrier, I was employed at a big-named investment company. I stuck it out for about five years until I got smart enough to realize I hated my life and who I worked for. I did a complete one-eighty and never regretted it once."

Elle nods at his words. "I'm beginning to feel the same way."

"Then you should move back." I surprise myself at the statement. Who am I to tell Elle what she should or shouldn't do?

She doesn't laugh like I think she will but, instead, rests her head in her hand. "What would I do? There aren't too many corporate accounting firms in Sandpoint."

"Come work for me." *Wow, let's shoot for the moon here, Oliver.*

Now her eyes widen. "Work for you? Doing what? Moving bags of manure? You know I have no experience in landscape development."

I shrug and try to act like I'm totally not stunned she's even entertaining this idea. "No, but I do pay somebody to take care of my finances. It's probably not enough to fill a full schedule, but I bet if you spread the word, you'd get tons of companies looking for someone to help with their accounting."

"Again, no business of mine, but that sounds like an idea worth pursuing," Bill says as he pushes back his chair. "I have thoroughly enjoyed meeting the both of you. And I appreciate your help with my puzzle." He makes a not-so-subtle nod toward Elle.

Yes, we all know I haven't put a single piece into place.

"But it's the top of the hour, so that means it's time for me to go take my pills." He reaches for the walker resting behind him and shuffles off.

"Old people are so funny," Elle says as we wave goodbye. "They're always so blunt."

"I'm sure it's because they've spent a lifetime being polite and subtle." I rub my hands up and down my pant legs. "They've finally learned that just saying what they think is the best approach." I wonder if I'll ever learn that lesson.

She nods and goes back to the puzzle.

I'm not quite ready to end this discussion. "So why *did* you move out to Denver in the first place? Why did you never come back to Sandpoint after college?"

Her hands still. "The job opportunity in Denver was too good to pass up." She grabs another piece and lifts it up as if studying it. Apparently, she doesn't realize she's holding it backward and is staring at the brown cardboard.

I have an inkling that the job wasn't her only reason for staying away from Sandpoint. "Any other factors?"

She lets out a slow breath and drops the piece in her hand. I brace myself as her eyes meet mine. "My family. I couldn't deal with living near my family anymore. I don't know if you've noticed, but they're overbearing and always in my business. Every time I have a decision to make, they're right there with their own opinions. I just...I just couldn't do it anymore."

We're silent for a minute, both of us lost in our own thoughts. I'm not shocked by her response. Everything she's said is true. But at the same time, I'm a little sad for her.

"Why did you never move?"

I lift my head to see her studying me. I don't even have to think about my answer. "Because of your family. Because they're completely overbearing and incessantly in my business. Because they always tell me their opinions about every aspect of my life, even when I don't ask for them." I can't hold back the small smile creeping across my face. "Because I know that I can turn to them at any moment. I know that I can depend on them for anything, and they'll be there."

She drops her hand from her chin, one corner of her mouth turned up. "I guess you're right. It's easy to forget the good things you have."

I think about Bill and his frankness. I think about the things I want to tell Elle but never have. Will I end up regretting these moments if I don't speak up?

Almost in slow motion, my hand reaches out for her palm resting on the table. Her fingers are cool, and I'm aware of the way her body jumps slightly at my touch. My words feel like they're building a blockade in my throat, protesting all attempts to get them out. I swallow hard. "Your family's awesome, Elle, but I'm not going to lie. It hasn't been the same since you left. It just feels like there's something—or someone—missing."

She looks down at my hand, her lips parted. What I wouldn't give to know every thought running through that mind of hers. It may just be my own hopefulness, but she doesn't seem repulsed by anything I've said.

"I...Oliver—"

"There you are," Elle's dad says, poking his head around the corner. "Heads up, everyone's leaving, and Mom wants to make sure you two get back home for the apple pies she and Auntie Lisa made all afternoon." Without another word, without even a meaningful glance at us huddled close together, her dad ducks out of the room.

That's what I like about Drew. He's probably the only member of his family that knows when to mind his own business.

Elle has pulled her hand back, and instead of finishing her thought, she stands, giving me a bright and extremely fake smile. "I guess we better get going."

Chapter 10 - Elle

It's official. I am going to ruin Christmas this year.

I look down at the pan of blackened caramel sauce and cringe. This is going to be the first Christmas Eve in, like, four hundred years that the Carter family does not have sticky toffee pudding for dessert.

Does anyone even like sticky toffee pudding? Honestly, no. But will anyone notice if the sticky toffee pudding isn't there? Absolutely. If there is one thing my family loves, it's their traditions.

And here I am, the Grim Reaper of the toffee-pudding-cake tradition.

I double-check the cupboard one more time to confirm that we are actually out of sugar. Yep. Flour, dry cereal, an absurd amount of hot cocoa mix...but no sugar.

On one hand, I shouldn't be held accountable for this disaster. It's my mom's fault. Who doesn't have copious amounts of sugar in stock over Christmas break?

On the other hand, this is my third ruined batch of the caramel sauce, so it isn't like I was judicious with the sugar we did have.

On the bright side, I now know about fifty ways to get burnt sugar off of a pan—thank you, Google.

Why did I offer to take care of the dessert for my mom again? Sure, I was trying to be helpful. The yeast in her triple batch of homemade rolls didn't rise, and it'd been too late to start the process over again. I swear she almost cried tears of joy when I had volunteered to make the cake as she dashed out the door for the grocery store.

It's almost funny now that she was so stressed about ruining Christmas with store-bought rolls. Little did she know, I'd be taking care of that with this failure of a pudding.

I massage my temples, thinking of all the options. Everyone in my family and extended family is already gathered at Auntie Lisa's house. I could call one of my aunties and ask to borrow some sugar, but if I tell them, my mom will hear about it within about two minutes. Most likely, she'll come rushing home from the store, trying to salvage the whole mess. I could call Autumn, but she's busy enough wrangling her two kids. I could run over to the store, but the timer on my oven says I only have twenty minutes until the cake comes out. There's no way I'm leaving that thing to burn too.

I moan and rest my head on the cool countertop. Maybe I can just bring a bag of chocolate chips? Heaven knows they're one of my favorite treats.

Then, an idea hits. Oliver.

I can call Oliver and ask him to bring me over some sugar from his mom's house. He'd be discreet enough that no one would know.

I glance at the clock, knowing I don't have time to debate the issue. I pull out my phone and quickly text him.

Elle: Hey, do you think I could borrow some sugar from your mom's house? Are you already over at Auntie Lisa's?

Oliver: Yes, but I can run home and grab some. Are you at your parents'?

Elle: Yes and thank you.
Elle: Also, can you try to not let anyone else know what you're doing? I'm making the sticky toffee pudding, and things are going south.
Elle: But don't worry, I'm totally fixing it. It'll be fine.

Oliver: Be still my heart. Not the sticky toffee pudding.

Elle: Do you even like sticky toffee pudding?

Oliver: Of course not. I'm more of a pumpkin pie kinda man.
Oliver: It's the principle of the matter. Plus, your mom will freak.

Elle: I know. That's why you need to be sneaky.

Oliver: Should I put on my spy outfit?

Elle: You're so dumb.
Elle: Do you have a spy outfit?

Oliver: Wouldn't you like to know?

I'm trying not to laugh at his text as I put the latest pan of ruined caramel sauce in the sink and fill it with hot water.

I haven't seen Oliver all day—something I know I should be grateful for, especially considering yesterday's unfortunate situation with the flowers (and there I'd been, thinking I was so clever sending myself roses). But strangely, I'm anything but grateful. I miss Oliver.

Less than five minutes later, he comes through the door, a ten-pound bag of sugar in his arms.

"Wow," I say, pretending to eye the bag but mostly just checking out Oliver—why miss an opportune moment? "When you let someone borrow a cup of sugar, you really give them a cup of sugar."

He grins and drops the goods on my counter. "I wasn't sure how much you needed. This is the sticky toffee pudding we're talking about." He sends me a knee-melting grin, and I'm suddenly grateful for the counter that separates us.

He's dressed up tonight—well, dressed up for Oliver. He's wearing this rust-colored sweater that must have shrunk slightly in the wash, because I swear it wasn't meant to fit shoulders his size. On the bright side, it gives me a great view of his toned upper body. The dark pants he has on are a step up from his usual jeans. Although, I'm not going to lie, I have no problem with his jeans either. He's even combed his hair tonight, which can only be because his mom came at him with a brush, or because he's trying to impress someone. Is that someone me?

My wrist suddenly feels cold, and I realize I've been squeezing the sponge in my hand tight enough to make water run down my arm. Enough daydreaming. I have a job to do.

"All right, hand it over," I say, reaching my arms out for the bag.

Instead of passing it to me, he picks it up and walks around until he's in the kitchen. So much for the safety net of the counter.

"So, what are we doing?" he asks, his fingers already pulling open the sugar.

I grab a clean pan and set it out. "We're making the caramel sauce that gets poured on top. I've screwed it up three times, so I'm pretty sure I know exactly what not to do."

"You really know how to spark confidence in a person."

I scowl before grabbing the measuring cup. "Enough chit-chat." I measure out the sugar and water, saying a silent prayer to the caramel gods to make this one work.

Oliver props one hip against the counter and folds his arms in a manly, grizzly-bear kind of stance that would seem intimidating if he didn't have that little half-smile on his face. "You realize you're holding your breath, don't you?"

I try to let out the giant breath of air I've been holding as imperceptibly as possible. "No, I'm not," I say when I've been fully deflated. I ignore his dimpled smirk. "Okay, now the key is to stir this for the first five minutes until the sugar is all dissolved. After that"—I hold my hands up in the air—"we cannot touch it until it hits three hundred and fifty degrees."

"What happens if we touch it?" Oliver whispers.

"The baking gods will come down and smite your caramel sauce so that it gets all grainy. Or else it'll scorch the bottom. Or it will turn rock hard. Or maybe they have more tricks up their sleeve that I haven't seen yet. All I know is, I'm not supposed to do it."

He holds his hand out for a fist bump. "We can do this."

He's being ridiculous, but I'm being a little ridiculous too, so I reach out and fist bump him just as the first bubbles start popping up in the water.

I grab my whisk and stir.

To keep my nerves at bay—and because I secretly love the sound of Oliver's voice—I ask about his day. "How was wood chopping? I'm assuming no one got hurt?" That morning, my dad had taken Oliver and my brothers out to chop wood for some of the elderly neighbors on our street.

"No one but the twins' pride," he says, reaching into the sink to scrub out the last pan of caramel I ruined.

Did the gesture make my heart melt a little? Yes. What can I say? I'm a softie for a man who cleans.

"Your dad put them in a chopping contest, and Logan smoked them both."

I laugh. "Serves those two right. They need a little humbling." And because I can't help asking, I say, "And what about you? You weren't part of the competition?"

He turns, giving me a wink. "The first competition was me against everyone. Let's just say years of landscaping has kept me in prime wood-chopping shape."

Obviously. I eye the sweater that is quickly becoming my favorite piece of clothing. My face heats up, but I'm blaming it on the steaming water in front of me. Definitely has nothing to do with the physique of my neighborhood friend that I have absolutely no romantic interest in—a point I seem to have a hard time remembering.

"Did you miss me?"

His question does nothing to help my flushed-face situation. "Miss you? Everyone misses you, Oliver. You're the only male under fifty in this family who can carry on an intelligent conversation."

He wipes his soapy hands on a towel, leaning in close. "I know, but did *you* miss me?"

There's no avoiding the meaning in this question.

"I—uh..." I swallow. Did I miss Oliver today? Yes. Every fiber of my body screams yes. I missed his calming presence, the way he can make any situation feel lighthearted with that little grin of his. I missed seeing him interact with my family, the way he intuitively knows when my mom needs someone to empty the trash for her or when my dad needs someone to listen to his opinion on a ref's call. I missed the way he looks at me like I am everything. Like insignificant little me makes his whole world go round.

The timer on my phone goes off, and I use my fumbling to wipe off my whisk as my excuse not to answer.

Unfortunately, Oliver must be on a mission tonight, because he just moves on to another uncomfortable question. "So, tell me more about that ring your brothers found yesterday."

Could we go back to talking about if I missed him or not today? "Oh yeah, ha ha. Wasn't that crazy?" Now that I'm no longer stirring, I have nothing to do with my hands. I grab a rag and start wiping the clean counter. "Who knows what other stuff was left in that closet?" My laugh feels forced, and I'm sure it sounds that way too.

Oliver is back to leaning on the cabinets like the cool, calm cucumber he is. Could he do me a favor and act a *little* flustered? I can't be the only one with beads of sweat forming on my back.

"I was just wondering why you kept it."

"Kept what?" Maybe if I play dumb, he'll give up.

"Kept the ring. You know, the one we're discussing."

Fine. Call my bluff. I wave my hand in the air. "I don't even know. It was just in my box of random mementos. I'm such a packrat. I'm not surprised it was in there." My arm is grabbed mid-wave, and even though his grip is soft, I feel powerless to pull away from him.

"If there's one thing I know, it's that you aren't a packrat, Elle Carter. Your favorite thing to do is throw away junk." His hand slides down my wrist until it's cradling my palm.

I'm staring at our hands, the way our fingers seem to intertwine so perfectly. I've never once held Oliver's hand before this weekend, but somehow, it feels like the most natural, wonderful thing in the world.

"So, I want to know why, out of all the knick-knacks in your life, you chose to save my ring."

My mouth goes dry. *Why?* Why did I choose to save a flimsy little piece of jewelry Oliver Moore gave me? I feel like the answer should be obvious.

"Do you want me to tell you about something I've kept for years?"

It takes me a second to register his question since I'm so lost in my own thoughts. "What?"

He reaches into his pocket, sliding out a brown, leather wallet that looks worn around the edges. "This might be one of my biggest, most embarrassing secrets ever," he says, flipping it open. "But considering the amount of pestering our families have given you about me, you deserve to see this." His fingers pull out a small photo that looks like the kind you'd get from those glamour photo booths at the mall.

He flips the picture around, and it's a headshot of a girl with a mouth full of metal braces and frizzy hair in need of a good deep-conditioning treatment.

I reach out and snag the photo from him, sirens going off in my head. "Oh my gosh." My jaw is on the floor. "Where did you...this is an absolutely hideous photo of me."

He throws his head back and treats me to one of his infectious laughs. "I can say that wasn't how I thought you'd react."

As I try to get over the fact that those middle-school days were some of the worst of my life, I notice some details I missed at first. The picture is well-worn around the edges as if it has been taken out and looked at numerous times. I can feel texture on the back and flip it over to see the words, *Have a great summer, Oliver!* written in a hot-pink gel pen.

"What year was this?"

His laughter has subsided by now, and he's staring intently at me. "It was your seventh grade and my eighth-grade year. You were handing out school photos to all your friends, and somehow, I managed to get one."

I don't remember this, which is strange since basically every detail of my life that involved Oliver is burned into my memory. I come back full circle to what we were talking about and use his own question on him. "Why did you save this?"

One hand comes up and rakes through his hair, disheveling the combed locks. "Elle, that's what I want to talk to you about. These last few days..." His voice trails off as if he's trying as hard as I am to collect his thoughts. "For years, I have ignored my attraction to you. No, more than that. I've stuffed it down so deep inside of me that neither I nor anyone else would ever know it existed. Because as much as I cared for you, as much as I was—am—attracted to you, I knew you didn't feel the same way about me. I knew it was one-sided." His eyes crinkle a little at the corners. "Despite your family's best attempts."

I don't think he's noticed his grip on my hand has tightened.

"But these last couple days...I don't know, maybe I'm just being an idiot. Maybe I'm reading into things more than I should."

His gaze meets mine like he wants me to intervene, but I'm having a hard time breathing, let alone talking.

"I feel like there have been moments," he continues. "Small, tiny moments where I wondered if I've misjudged your feelings all along. Maybe you don't think of me as just the annoying neighbor your family tries to swindle you into dating."

His thumb is stroking the back of my hand, sending tingles up and down my arm.

"Maybe you're not as indifferent to me as I thought."

This is one of those big moments. The fork in the road. The diverging paths. The time when I really need to weigh my options and make a life-changing decision.

I hate life-changing decisions.

My eyes study the face I'm so familiar with. Black-brown eyes and deep laugh lines. Cheeks lined with scruff I've dreamed of running my fingers through to see if it's prickly or soft. Those heart-stopping dimples and strong jawline that, as Sophie stated, really *would* improve anyone's gene pool.

This is a man with a heart of gold. A man who is kind and hardworking and good to his core. A man who is asking me to finally, after all this time, be honest with him.

My legs feel like soup, and there are not delicate butterflies but a horde of rambunctious pigeons in my stomach. "Oliver, that ring... I kept that ring because it was a tie to you. It was something from you that was all mine. Something none of my family planned out or coerced you into giving me." I let out a shaky breath. "It was something I knew was real."

He tilts his head. "When have I ever been anything but real with you?"

"It's not that I think you haven't been real." My body is experiencing a series of hot flashes, but there are goosebumps on both my arms, and I suddenly have a new appreciation for those years of menopause my mom went through. "It's just that it's never been only us. It's always been my zoo of a family stepping in, making sly remarks, and pushing you toward me. I don't know, I think I just wanted something that I knew was one hundred percent about me. I wanted someone who pursued me and loved me on their own. And I don't...I don't know if I can ever have that with you." I hang my head, feeling like I should pull away but wanting to stay close to him. "I know this sounds ridiculous and juvenile, and it probably is. But at least it's honest."

At some point, he must've slipped his arm around me, because one hand tightens on my back as the other cradles my cheek. Everything about him is so warm and solid. So comfortable.

"Elle, I know it seems like your family is always in the middle of everything. I understand that you question if anything I do is my own choice or something set up by one of them. But I can promise you, all my feelings, all my thoughts about you are mine. I love your family, and I hope I'm always close to them, but they are nothing to me compared to you." His eyes shut for a split second, as if he's gearing himself up for something. "But I want the same from you. I want to know that if none of your family were involved, and it was just you and me, you'd feel the same way."

Our faces are inches away, our breaths intermingling. He has that fresh cologne smell I have categorized as the best scent in the world, and the soft fabric of his sweater is surrounding me like a warm blanket. All it would take is for me to lift my head an inch, and our mouths would meet.

My soul is singing yes. Every gravitational force in the world is working on me, pulling my body toward his. But ten years of reservations, ten years of suppressing my feelings is a hard hurdle to get over, and I hesitate.

My phone starts ringing on the counter, its vibrations like an annoying fly buzzing around the room. I ignore it. I don't have the mental capacity right now to speak to my mom or aunties or whoever the heck is trying to reach me.

Unfortunately, whoever's on the other end doesn't feel the same. There's a second when the buzzing stops, and I say, "Oliver—"

Then the buzzing starts up again, and I curse out loud.

Oliver drops one of my hands, a hint of a smile on his lips. "It must be important," he says, reaching for the phone. He picks it up and looks at the screen, and I can literally see the moment he shuts down. With a face carved like a slab of cold stone, he offers it to me, screen side up.

Across it, I can see the name *Danny* in black letters.

"Looks like your boyfriend wants to talk to you," Oliver says, dropping my hand and stepping back.

I've always heard that description where a situation makes someone freeze up, but this is the first time I've ever experienced the sensation in real life. My body can't move. Every nerve, every muscle is in this limbo state of indecision.

Oliver clearly doesn't have that problem as he turns away. "Looks like you've got everything handled here. I'll see you back at Auntie Sharon's house."

And then he's gone.

*****

I've spent almost all of Christmas Eve, one of my favorite nights of the year, in a haze.

I did successfully finish the caramel sauce (and learned that if you really want to master a recipe, the key is to botch it up a few times beforehand). But other than that,

I've spent most of the evening keeping myself busy. My auntie's house is a circus, giving no opportunity for the deep introspection I'm in desperate need of. And there is no way I am ready to talk to Oliver without thinking things through.

Luckily, my mom and aunties are so concerned with getting the meal perfect they don't waste any breath on me as I dutifully chop herbs and stir last-minute sauces while they flit around the kitchen like a bunch of squawking hens.

Oliver must have a similar plan to mine since he's kept himself engaged in various activities all night, all on opposite sides of the room from me.

Unfortunately for him, I know his nervous ticks. His knuckle cracking is on overdrive, and he's run his fingers through his hair so many times, it's almost standing straight up. Who can blame him, though? It isn't exactly like I'm bounding over there, trying to fix the giant spit wad I've turned our lives into.

After dinner, I'm the first to volunteer for dish duty.

"Are you sure those rolls didn't ruin the meal?" my mom asks as she walks into the kitchen a few minutes later.

This is probably the fifteenth time tonight she's asked me this. I plunge another pan into the soapy sink in front of me. "Mom, the rolls were delicious. If you hadn't told me they were store bought, I'd have no idea." I lift my eyebrows. "I'm still surprised you were able to find them on such late notice, though."

She becomes very preoccupied with folding dish towels in front of her.

"Mom? How did you get these rolls?"

She waves her hand at me. "Don't worry about it. But as advice, if you ever find yourself in a sticky situation, having a few Benjamins on hand never hurts when dealing with the bakery department."

I barely hold back my laugh. Only my mom would bribe the bakery staff on Christmas Eve.

"Also, you did a great job with the sticky toffee pudding. Much better than Auntie Lisa did last year, but don't tell her I said that."

I shake my head and grab another pan. "Mum's the word."

The woman in question walks into the kitchen with Auntie Sharon in tow. "Ladies, I don't want to toot our own horns, but that was a successful meal if I've ever served one." She dumps a mile-high stack of dirty plates next to me, and I'm suddenly regretting my decision to be on dish duty.

"Even Autumn had two servings—she's always such a lightweight—and Oliver told me they were the best scalloped potatoes he's ever had."

We all make the appropriate cheering sounds at her declaration.

"Speaking of Oliver," Auntie Sharon says, leaning against the counter like she's settling in for a lengthy conversation, "whatever happened to the two of you yesterday at the retirement villa?" She wiggles her eyebrows. "One second you were harmonizing with me to "Silent Night," and the next second, both you and he were gone. A snoopier person might wonder what the two of you were doing."

I don't know if it's possible to find a snoopier person, but I hold that opinion back. I need to nip this in the bud because I'm not in a state of mind to deal with any kind of teasing right now. "One of the assistants asked if we could help in the game room. They were a little short-staffed and wanted a few more people to entertain the members." Okay, maybe that's a bit of a white lie, but sometimes the end justifies the means. "Absolutely nothing interesting whatsoever happened."

There must be an edge to my tone, because my mom makes a gesture with her right hand across her throat.

Auntie Lisa picks up the conversation by telling a story about her son's latest basketball game.

I go back to washing. Maybe I made up the part about a worker asking for Oliver's and my help, but besides that, everything I said was completely true. Nothing *had* happened between him and me—not yesterday, nor any other time before then. And it was all because of me.

I think about the way he had looked at me tonight, the way his eyebrows knit together and his mouth pressed into that thin line when he picked up my phone.

Has my family been right all along? Have their years of pushing Oliver and me together been because we actually are perfect for each other?

I like to think I'm a level-headed person. That I weigh the pros and cons before making decisions and passing judgments. But maybe this time I've let my pride get in the way. Maybe my reluctance to let my family help, to listen to their advice, has gotten in the way of me seeing how right they are. Because at the end of the day, it isn't like their influence really matters. Oliver and I are adults and can make decisions for ourselves.

So why am I using them as my excuse?

I look across the room, finding Oliver setting up a game of chess with my Uncle Marlo. I think back to the way he played dinosaurs with my nephews before dinner so Autumn could get a break. The way he listened to my cousin Logan talk for half the meal about his career as a video gamer—and I use the term *career* very loosely. The way he complimented my mom and aunts on all the food, bringing that blush of pride to each of their faces.

He's perfect.

He's everything I could ever hope for.

And I'm done being ridiculous about this whole situation. I'm done holding back.

I drop the stack of plates into the sink, resulting in a tidal wave of soapy water splashing onto the counter.

My mom grabs a double fist of dish towels. "You okay, Elle?" she asks, her mouth pressed into a worried line.

I give her a wide smile, the first one I've felt like handing out all night. "Yes, I think I'm actually going to be okay."

*****

Thinking I'm going to do something and actually doing it are two completely different things.

I spend the rest of the evening doing this bob-and-weave kind of dance with Oliver. *I'm* trying to find an opportunity where we can be at least semi-alone, and I'm pretty confident *he* is doing the complete opposite.

We watch the latest version of *The Grinch Who Stole Christmas*, play a rousing (if somewhat tipsy game of charades), listen to my dad read the Christmas story from the Bible (that he decides to paraphrase two verses in), and even put out round two of desserts for everyone, and still, there is no opening for me to talk with Oliver.

It's not until Autumn finally claims that her boys need to get to bed before Santa comes that people make any moves to leave.

I'm watching Oliver like a hawk, waiting for him to make a move toward the door so I can pounce.

"Oliver, I think it's time for us to get going too," his mom says, and I could almost kiss her—until I realize I need a reason to break the two of them apart without being too obvious. The sugar.

"Oh, Oliver," I say, stepping toward them, "why don't you stop by our house on your way home, and I can give you back the sugar I borrowed."

Lauren makes an unsteady halt at my voice. "What sugar?"

I'm already slipping on my shoes. "I had to borrow some for the sticky toffee pudding. Oliver brought it to me earlier today." I purposely do not look Oliver in the face because I'm a chicken and can't bear to wonder what he's thinking just now. All three of us walk outside, the cold night air making my lungs clench up. "I'll run ahead and grab the sugar," I say, hoping this buys enough time for Oliver to walk his mom to her door.

The stars must align, because as I stumble out my parents' door three minutes later with a ten-pound bag in my arms, Oliver is standing on my doorstep alone.

This is it. Time for my speech.

Once again, my mind performs its newly cultivated skill of going completely blank.

Oliver's hands reach out for the bag, his fingers cold as they brush across mine.

"T-thanks again for coming to my rescue," I finally get out.

"No problem."

That's it. No smile, no wink, no neighborly joke about borrowing a cup of sugar. My resolve is weakening.

"Oliver, about my boyfriend, about when we were talking—"

"Elle, don't worry about it. It's water under the bridge." I can barely make out his eyes, but they're staring at a point on the wall somewhere above my shoulder. "Tell Danny I said Merry Christmas."

With that, he steps off the porch, his stride strong and confident like he knows exactly where he's going in life and what his plans are.

I lean against the door frame, feeling the complete opposite.

Chapter 11 - Oliver

It's like I'm waking up the morning after one of my college parties. The kind where you're wondering if everything from the night before really happened or if it was just a dream.

I roll over, my feet getting caught in the bed covers for a second. It's the same way I feel about my relationship with Elle. Trapped.

Where am I supposed to go from here? Clearly, there's no romantic path ahead of us, but I can't imagine going back to just being her friendly, platonic neighbor that she sees on random holidays and family functions.

I kick my legs free. It's my own fault. I've been so stupid. I've spent the last thirty years ignoring my feelings for Elle—well, maybe not ignoring, but at least never acting on them—then she gives me half a second of attention, and I go and blow it all.

It's just...this is the first time Elle has ever seemed to reciprocate anything. In high school, she was immune to any of my good manners or charm. (Although, to be fair, it was high school, so I'm sure I wasn't as charming as I thought.)

But at the tree lighting, something seemed to shift between us. Then, there was our conversation at the retirement villa. There had been sparks on her end too, hadn't there? I'd almost combusted with the emotions rolling through my body. And then there was the ring she'd kept. For anybody else, it might seem a pointless, random thing, but nothing Elle ever does is random. There's a reason she kept my ring, and apparently, I decided last night was the time to get answers.

I look at the window, noting it's still dark outside. Grabbing my pillow, I fluff it out and then jam it under my head.

It's fine. Elle and I are both leaving tomorrow anyway. The key is to just get through today, acting as normal as possible.

For probably the fifty-eighth time, I second-guess the gift I left under her tree yesterday. I had dropped it off when I brought the sugar by. I should've grabbed it on my way out once I realized things were over for us, but it'd slipped my mind.

For some reason, a small part of me doesn't want to take it back. I want Elle to have it.

I shake my head and drop another pillow on top of my face. Sometimes I really am a sentimental sap, aren't I?

Chapter 12 - Elle

The good thing about having a house full of adults on Christmas morning is that nobody's waking up at the crack of dawn to open presents.

Unless you happen to be me.

Although, it has nothing to do with what Santa's put under the tree. I'm going to let Oliver take the credit for this bout of insomnia.

I look at the time on my phone. Five-thirty. I wonder if Sophie's awake.

Obviously, she's not, and a good friend wouldn't bother her, but I must not be a very good friend.

I open our text thread.

Elle: SOS

It's at least a minute before she responds, and I can just imagine her rolling over in bed, cursing slightly as she realizes what time it is.

Sophie: You'd better be dying to be texting me this early.

Elle: Does it count if I'm emotionally dying?

Sophie: No.

I grin and ignore her.

Elle: Last night Oliver and I were alone because I'd messed up the caramel for the sticky toffee pudding and I needed more sugar so I asked

him to bring me some from his mom's house while everyone else was at my aunt's house.

Sophie: That has to be one of the longest run-on sentences I've ever seen. I almost died from lack of oxygen reading that out loud.
Sophie: Also, you're having a nervous breakdown because you were alone with the man of your dreams? This doesn't feel worthy of a 5 AM text to your best friend.
Sophie: Ex-best friend. I'm pretty sure you woke me in the middle of my REM stage of sleep.

Elle: I wasn't done. I hit enter too soon. And it's 5:30, not 5 AM. Anyway, Oliver hit me with all these questions about why I still have his ring and how I feel about him, and I didn't know what to say!

Sophie: So what did you say?

Elle: I don't even know! Some gibberish about not knowing if his feelings for me were real or if they were the result of my family pushing me at him for fifteen years.

Sophie: Well, that's a ridiculous argument. He's a grown man, Elle. Your family's opinions are not the driving force of his decisions.

Elle: Thank you for your support. I feel so much better now.
Elle: Also, you've never met my family. They can be very persuasive. But that's not even the worst part. The worst part is when you called last night—sorry, I just realized I never called you back—it was right in the middle of his big

declaration. I'm about 95% sure he was about to kiss me.

Elle: Maybe 87% sure.

Sophie: What???

Sophie: He almost kissed you, and you let a dumb phone call get in the way??

Sophie: And I accept your apology for not calling me back. I was only slightly offended.

Elle: He was the one that picked up the phone. And the worst part is he didn't know it was you. He thought it was my fake boyfriend because I changed your name to Danny in case anyone looked through my contacts.

Sophie: First off, that is like the third time you've said "the worst part is." You need to get your story straight. And second off, who is going to look up your boyfriend's name on your phone?

Elle: Clearly you don't have brothers. The point is, he cut and ran after that.

Sophie: Okay, okay. Let's think this through. I think you need to find Oliver today—probably wait a few hours because he might not be as forgiving as your best friend if you wake him up this early— and have a serious talk with him. Tell him that you don't have a boyfriend, and you actually love him and want to be the mother of his children.

Elle: I'm not saying that.

Elle: Also, are we back to best-friend status?

Sophie: It's how you feel, isn't it?

Sophie: Maybe.

My fingers hover over the keyboard. She's right. I do love Oliver. And I think I've loved him for a long time.

Elle: Yes.

Sophie: Then what's the problem?

Elle: I don't think he feels the same way about me anymore.

I lay my head back against my pillow, its cushion no help in soothing my aching head. I just need to get up and move around. Lying here, ulcerating about this, is doing me no good.

Elle: Now that I've properly woken you up, I'm going to leave you alone. Go back to dreaming of sugarplums or whatever it is Santa's going to leave in your stocking.

Sophie: I'd be happy with a Visa gift card.

I send her a smiley face then tuck my phone away. What I need is a cup of hot chocolate. Nothing soothes troubles like a dose of sugar. Plus, I'm freezing.

I grab my pair of leggings from last night and find one of those chunky sweaters my mom hates in my suitcase.

I make quick work of heating up some milk in the microwave. Lucky for me, my mom has a serious addiction to gourmet hot chocolate, so I end up with a raspberry-truffle flavor.

Five minutes later, I'm settling into one of the oversized armchairs in our living room, facing the glowing Christmas tree. It's funny to me that my mom puts the tree in here since it's the smallest and least-used room in our house, but she says she loves seeing it twinkling through the front windows.

I stare at the way the lights bounce off the bulbs and jumble of ornaments. I remember being a kid and arguing relentlessly with my brothers about who got to put up which ornaments. It's shocking to think it's been years since I've decorated a Christmas tree. Is that who I'm becoming? The distant family member that occasionally shows up to holidays or get-togethers? Am I ever going to settle down and have traditions and a family of my own?

A noise to my right makes me jump until I see my dad shuffling into the room with a blanket thrown over his shoulders.

"You're up early," he says, easing into the other armchair.

"I just love looking at the tree like this." As a matter of fact, it was my dad's and my tradition to be the first to come and sit in front of the tree on Christmas mornings. I can't believe I'd forgotten that. He used to always say it was our special time to count the presents and make sure we got the most out of everyone. A smile fills my face at the memory.

"Which flavor did you make?" He points to my steaming cup.

"Raspberry truffle. Although, I was waffling between that and the salted caramel."

He nods, leaning back into the chair. "Those are both solid choices. I recommend staying clear of the white-chocolate one—has a weird aftertaste."

I take a small sip, savoring the rich, silky flavor on my tongue. "Mom's collection is getting a little out of control. You almost need to build her a cabinet just for hot chocolate mixes."

His eyes are closed but he smiles. "I know. But they make her happy. And I've learned that whatever makes her happy makes me happy."

For not the first time in my life, I think that I want a relationship like my parents' one day. A relationship filled with love and respect and an equal concern for the other person.

"Elle, are you doing okay?"

The question surprises me. My dad, while one of the best of men, usually stays out of any family drama. I bring the cup to my chin, letting the steam warm my face. "Yeah, I'm fine." I allow myself a quick glance and see him studying me.

"It's just that everybody's been a little pushy this last week with you and Oliver. I'm sorry about that. I know it makes things uncomfortable for you."

I smile, both grateful and sad to see the worry lines creasing his brow. "They are a little over the top, but it's nothing I can't handle."

He nods, but those worry lines don't go away.

I can see tufts of snow falling softly outside, a glow of the rising sun highlighting the flurry of snowflakes. If only I could freeze this moment and live in the peaceful quiet instead of the chaos my life has become the last few days. "Dad, is there anything you've ever regretted not doing in life?" Given the way his eyebrows shoot up, I've surprised him just as much as I've surprised myself by the question.

"Regret...is there anything I regret?" The blanket falls from his shoulders, but he doesn't seem to notice. "I still wish I had tried out for the basketball team in college. I'm sure I never would've seen any game time, but I wish I would've tried." He rubs one hand absentmindedly up and down his flannel pajama bottoms. "Other than that, though, I don't think there's much. I learned early on to always go for the things I want. Your mother taught me that lesson. She's always been a go-getter. She told me that you never get what you want by sitting back, and I guess I've taken that to heart."

I nod but don't reply. His words are sweeping over me on repeat, kinda like my washing machine every time I forget to move the clothes to the dryer. Is that how I'll feel about Oliver for the rest of my life? Will I regret giving up?

There's rustling behind us again, and I turn to see Rhett, one hand rubbing his eyes as he lets out a long yawn. "Have you guys shaken all the presents already?"

A second later, Brett is behind him, shoving his twin out of the way. "Just so everyone knows, I counted them, and I have the most." He glances at me with sad eyes that I know are fake. "Sorry, Elle, you're on the low end of the totem pole. Apparently, someone hasn't been a very good girl this year."

I chuck a pillow at him, which he uses to cushion his head as he sprawls out on the floor.

One by one, the rest of my family trickles in. My brother with his sons, both still in that magical, awestruck age when it comes to Christmas. Then, Autumn makes a debut with two cups of coffee in hand, one she hands to Noah. "It was a long night," is all she says as she slouches onto the couch.

Finally, even my mom comes downstairs, complete with rollers in her hair and her signature fuzzy robe. "Alright, everyone, here's how we'll do this," she says like she's directing traffic—which, considering she's managed the opening of Christmas presents going on thirty years now, that's probably what it feels like to her. She proceeds to give us all orders, which we obey without question.

An hour later, the room looks like a bomb of wrapping paper and boxes went off, and there are only a few more presents left straggling under the tree.

Rhett is wearing the set of hot-pink mittens and scarf I got him—Brett got a matching purple version—and is digging under the tree for the last gifts. "Here, Elle, there's one more for you." He lifts up a small box, peering at the name tag. His eyes go wide. "It's from Oliver."

If my track coach ever had any questions about my hurdling capabilities, he should've seen me now. Leaping across the room like a gazelle (or at least in my mind—I may or may not have squished several presents and people on my way), I tear the box from his hand.

As I stare at the gift tag, I can faintly hear my mom complaining in the background that I should've gotten a present for Oliver after all.

My fingers run over the smooth material of the box, the entire thing sitting in the palm of my hand. What could he have gotten me?

I block out the noises of the rest of my family. It's just me, this green box, and my trembling hands. I untie the white ribbon, ever so slowly lifting the lid before gasping at what I see inside.

Inside is a small metal ring. It's simple, really, just a silver band with the tiniest etching of a heart on one side. Underneath is a note.

I recognize Oliver's heavy-handed scrawl.

Elle,

Since it's been almost ten years, it's probably time you got an upgrade from the candy-dispenser ring I got you all those years ago.

I figure if you're going to keep a promise ring from me, it might as well be a proper promise ring.

Love, Oliver

I close my eyes and tilt my head forward, resting it on the box in front of me. What does this mean? Of all the times to be cryptic and cutesy, this is not it. And when did he put this under the tree? Given his parting words last night, it seems likely he put it there earlier yesterday. Had he meant to come take it back before I opened it?

I need answers.

"What is it?"

"I think it's a ring. I can't see. Her head is in the way."

"A ring? A *ring*?"

I come back to the present, an echo of my family's whispered (well, not whispered—words spoken at completely normal volume but said in a hissing tone) conversations behind me. I turn just as my mom pounces, grabbing my arm with the box.

"It *is* a ring! He proposed! We're having a wedding!" She starts dancing around the room, her hands thrown over her head. The rest of my family looks shocked, but it's a good kind of shock, like when you check out at the grocery store and realize their ice cream bars were actually buy one, get one free.

I need to put a stop to this immediately.

I hold my hands up high. "Wait, no. No. It's not an engagement ring!" I wave the note in the air, although I keep a firm hold on it because there's no way I'm letting any of them read it. "It's just a replacement for that plastic one he got me all those years ago. That's all."

My mom drops her hands, her eyebrows furrowed. "Wait, why would a man get you a ring if it's not an engagement ring? That's the most ridiculous thing I've—"

"Maybe he wants to start small," Rhett breaks in. "You know, start with the plastic ring, move on to a metal ring." He gives me a sly grin. "Maybe one day Elle will get upgraded to an actual diamond."

"No, there's got to be a step between a non-diamond ring and a diamond ring. Like a sapphire or something. Maybe a ruby?"

My twin brothers are loving this way too much.

My mom continues arguing that a ring is only proper for an engagement. Noah is pushing Autumn to get a closer look at the ring, and my two nephews are methodically emptying all the trash bags full of wrapping paper.

I ignore everything and turn to the one person in the room that has any sanity. My dad.

He's staring at me, his lips pursed together, the corners of his eyes crinkled like they do when he's thinking hard.

I step close, and he takes my hand with the box, turning it so he can see the ring inside. "You know, Elle, as I said earlier, you'll never get what you want by sitting back." He gives my hand a light squeeze. "Go after him, if that's what you want."

A heat spreads across my chest, and I realize he's right. I can't imagine a life without Oliver. Even though I keep trying to escape him, I always come back.

Before my reasonable, self-doubting side can break in, I spring up, charging out the front door with the little green box in hand. I'm crunching over the freshly fallen snow in my slippers that are definitely not waterproof, the icy air biting through my thin leggings and sweater.

Like some sort of crazy woman, I reach their door and bang on it hard. Once. Twice. Adrenaline is pumping through my body, and everything feels jittery, like I'm a popcorn kernel right before it bursts. I wait in silence for a few seconds, hearing nothing. Considering it's just Oliver and his mom, I'd be surprised if they were actually awake.

Luckily, that doesn't stop me. The handle is locked, so I resort to banging on the door again.

This time, I hear faint movement on the other side, a voice calling to me that they're coming. I see Oliver's face squinting through the glazed window on the side of the door, but I can't see his expression. Then, the handle turns.

He's standing in front of me, wearing nothing but a pair of jogger pants.

Nothing but a pair of jogger pants.

I mean, I'm sure I've seen Oliver with his shirt off before. Obviously. But it was back in, like, seventh grade. This chiseled chest and one, two, three, four...too many abs to count were certainly not present during those games of Marco Polo in the community pool. He shifts, and I decide right then that rippling muscles are most definitely my love language.

I don't know how long I've been staring mutely at him, but I do my best to hide the metaphorical drool running out of my mouth.

"Merry Christmas, Elle," Oliver says, his voice slightly groggy. "It's nice to see you so...bright and early."

I'm trying to get my voice to work, but I can't seem to think of anything to say. He leans against the door frame and folds his arms, which I think is a power play, because it makes his biceps appear even bigger and more intimidating. I'm here for it.

"Did Santa come to the Carter house this morning?" he asks with a stoic face.

Eyes off the chest, Elle. I swallow and close my eyes—there's less distraction that way. I tighten my fingers over the green box, its corners biting into my flesh. I lift it up, opening the lid so he can see the ring inside. "Were you serious about this?"

He looks at the box, his mouth pressing into a tight line. "What do you mean?"

"I mean," I say, opening my eyes and waving my hands in the air, "were you serious about this whole promise-ring thing? About the whole 'your feelings for me have always been real', and the tension-filled moments we've been having, and the two times I swear you've almost kissed me?" I'm pretty sure the entire neighborhood can hear me at this point, but I am on a one-way train with no plans of getting off. "I've never had such a roller coaster of emotions in my life than in the last three days. So, tell me straight, what is your purpose with this?" I hold the box higher so it's level with his nose.

Slowly, he reaches one hand out and wraps it around mine, lowering my arm until the box is back at my waist. "Elle, if you've been on an emotional roller coaster the last three days, that's one hundred percent on you. Because if there's one thing that's never changed, it's my feelings for you."

If I was hoping for a jaw-dropping confession, I think I just got it.

"If I ever thought there was a chance you reciprocated my feelings, you better believe I would've been begging you to have me. But if there's one thing *you've* been consistent about the last ten years, it's your obvious dislike of me."

His words feel like someone has just switched the salt and sugar in a batch of cookies. And the worst part is, he's right. I have gone out of my way to prove to him and my family that I am not in the slightest bit interested in gorgeous Oliver Moore.

He's still talking. "But something seemed different this trip. You've been different. It's like you finally opened the door to me a crack. And you better believe I was gonna stick my foot in there and hold it open."

I look down and realize he's holding both my hands. I don't even know when he grabbed the other one, but his thumbs are rubbing soft circles in my palms.

"Honestly, the only thing keeping me back is this boyfriend of yours. I've never disliked the name Danny so much until now." He gives me a tiny grin before it drops. "Because if you're with someone, I would never cross that boundary."

His words trail off, and I'm inhaling and exhaling like the world's oxygen levels have just been depleted. It's time. Time to fess up and be completely honest. This is going to be embarrassing. "He's fake." I don't add anything more, hoping he'll leave it at that.

"What?"

Dang it. "Danny. My boyfriend." I sigh. "I made him up because I was tired of my family pushing me at you. I thought that maybe if I had a boyfriend, they would leave it all alone." I chew my bottom lip, wondering if he thinks I'm crazy. "Which I now know is not a strong enough deterrent for them."

He smiles, and those stupid dimples that I love more than anything in the world are popping out of his cheeks.

"Your boyfriend is fake." The wheels in his head are almost visibly turning. "I'm assuming there's no one else in your life? No one real, that is?" He lifts his eyebrows.

I shake my head, still struggling with getting oxygen into my body even though I mastered this skill twenty-eight years ago.

He stares at me in silence, white puffs of air forming between us from our breaths. "If that's the case, my final question is"—he pauses for a split second—"what *are* your feelings about me?"

What are my feelings about Oliver? What can I say? That he is the most perfect man I've ever known? That he is kind and good and sweet and determined and every other positive adjective out there? Should I just sit here and pour out compliment after compliment on him? He probably deserves it after all the cold-shoulder years I've given him. I look in his eyes and see the vulnerability there.

No, I'll tell him the one thing I know he wants to hear.

"Oliver," I say, taking a step toward him, "you are the only one I have ever loved. You're the only one who can make me laugh hard enough to make me pee my pants. You are the only one that can drive me bonkers with your knuckle cracking and teasing, but never enough to make me truly angry. You're the only one in this world that can handle my crazy family and not run for the hills. You're the only one I've stalked online the last five years, desperate to know as much about you while seeming uninterested as possible." I take another step, obliterating any space between me and the hard, still-naked chest. I bring my arms up, resting them comfortably over his shoulders and around his neck. "You're the one I want to spend the rest of my life with," I say, my voice a soft whisper.

I don't know if I even finish that last word before his mouth is on mine. Strong arms are wrapped around me, crushing me to him as if he's afraid I'll escape. His kiss is bold and explosive, like he's been dreaming of this for years. Soft lips explore mine without hesitation, and I want it all.

I lean into him, needing to get closer despite the fact that there's not a molecule of space between us. My fingers comb through his hair, and as I inhale his familiar clean scent, I decide then and there he is never changing his brand of body wash for the rest of our lives.

It's only after a few seconds—or is it minutes? Hours?—that I hear it.

Cheering.

I pull back and look over my shoulder, not sure whether to laugh or cry at what's before me. Lined up in the snow like a bunch of news reporters is my family. My mom is crying into my dad's arms, and my brothers are whistling and yelling, "It's about time!" Noah is cheering in between dodging snowballs from his sons, and even Autumn has joined in my family's evil ways and is recording the entire thing on her phone.

I look back at Oliver who is grinning with no shame. He pumps his fist in the air and lets out one victory whoop before yanking me into his house and slamming the door.

"I am so sorry—" I begin to say, completely mortified, but he silences me with a kiss.

"Don't." He pulls back an inch. "You just gave your entire family—especially your mom—the best Christmas present ever." He smiles, his eyes still on my mouth. "But I think that was enough of a show for them. Now I want the rest of you to myself."

Just as he leans in again, there's the sound of footsteps.

"What is all the—oh my word! Is it finally happening?!" Oliver's mom's voice cries from behind him.

I don't think escaping our families is ever going to be a possibility.

Epilogue

"You know, for being a minimalist, you sure have a lot of stuff." Oliver grunts as he stacks another box by my door.

"All this *stuff* is going to be moving into your apartment in about one week," I say, wiggling my diamond-encrusted finger—courtesy of him—in the air. "So you better get used to it."

He groans but goes back for another box. "So, did you ever hear from that real estate company?" he calls from the other room.

I smile and look at the bare walls of what used to be my apartment. "Yes, they made me an offer yesterday."

I hear a whoop followed by a crashing noise.

"Are you breaking my stuff?" I holler back as I stick books into a box.

"You didn't like that picture frame anyway," he says as he walks back in.

I spring to my feet. "Oliver! If you're going to break everything—"

He silences my protest with a kiss, although I do put up a fight for at least half a second, which I think is admirable given his kissing abilities. Abilities I've sampled quite frequently over the last six months.

"So, with my landscaping business, the hardware store, and this real estate company, that should put you almost at max capacity in terms of work, right?"

I nod, my arms sliding around his waist. "Guess you're getting exactly what you wanted all along," I say, giving him a smirk. "Free accounting work."

"Not to mention a hot future wife. I'm a business-savvy kind of guy."

My front door swings open, and a loud voice calls out, "Reinforcements have arrived—oh, ew, gross! Can you two get a room or something?"

I roll my eyes as Rhett makes a show of covering his. I walk over and give my little—even though he's actually a head taller than me—brother a hug. "One day, I'll teach you about the birds and the bees. But for now, thank you for coming to help."

He slings an arm around me and returns my squeeze. "I know Oliver is getting a little up there in years. I don't want him to strain his back from carrying a frying pan or anything."

Oliver reaches over and tackles my brother into a headlock just as there's another knock on my front door. Actually, Rhett just barged in, so I guess this is the first knock.

On the other side is Sophie with a bag of steaming food in one hand and a roll of packing tape in the other. "I know, I know, you can thank me for the foresight of bringing lunch later," she says, stopping short when she sees the wrestling match going on in my empty living room.

"Thanks so much for coming." I turn and snap my fingers at Oliver and Rhett. "Hey, can you two stop acting like five-year-olds for a second?"

Oliver is the first to pop his head up. "Hi, Sophie." He gives Rhett a final shove as he gets to his feet.

Rhett rolls over, and I know the minute his eyes land on my stunning friend, because they go as wide as those frying pans he was talking about.

In one move, he hops up, one hand stretched out and a playful grin on his face. "Well, hello. I had no idea the rest of the moving company was so attractive. It's good to know Oliver's ugly mug isn't the only thing I'm going to have to stare at all afternoon."

Sophie's face has gone this cute shade of pink, and I can tell she doesn't know how to respond.

I'll save her. "Sophie," I say, purposely pushing my brother back a step, "this is my brother, Rhett. He is gracing us with his presence to help me move. Rhett," I say, putting an edge in my words in hopes that he'll stop acting like his usual self, "this is my best friend in the world, Sophie." An idea comes to my mind, and I can't stop the smile that spreads across my face. "Although, you know her more formally as Danny."

Rhett's eyes narrow for a minute before widening in understanding. He sends Sophie a wink. "Sophie, I've never been happier to meet one of my sister's acquaintances."

The End

Thank You!!

Thank you so much for reading! This book was one of my favorites to write so far. I come from a big family and knew I wanted to include a bunch of siblings and extended family members that were totally in Elle and Oliver's business. Because honestly, who doesn't love an annoying younger brother or overbearing aunt that has to know everything about everyone?

I also have a little bit of Elle's stubbornness in me so I may or may not have written some of this from the heart. :) Sometimes accepting that others know what's best for you is a tough pill to swallow. Ha ha!

Did you know that reviews help me SO much? If you have a second, I would love to hear what you thought on an Amazon review!

To know about my latest books, (and to get a free book!) sign up for my exclusive New Release Mailing List here: www.summerdowell.com

Also by Summer Dowell

It's Just Business: The Wedding Business Series
If It's Perfect: The Wedding Business Series

A Temporary Engagement: The Fake Love Series
A Temporary Boyfriend: The Fake Love Series
A Temporary Marriage: The Fake Love Series

Love From Scratch
A Run at Love

About The Author

Meet Summer. Your best-reading-bud-that-you've-never-actually-met who's obsessed with writing romance books. You know, that friend that always has a sarcastic comeback and whose favorite thing is to sit next to you on the couch, not talking, reading our own books? That's Summer.

She's a stay home mom to 6 and has a slight need to escape the laundry and diaper chaos. Summer turned her ability to see the humor in anything into a lineup of books that now inspire readers to chuckle, snicker, and even lol at the embarrassing situations she puts characters in.

Her superpower? Besides writing book dedications that purposely call out her husband, she is really good at giving people an escape from their everyday lives in the form of a story.

Made in United States
Orlando, FL
16 June 2024